Dear Reader,

You have no idea how much I appreciate you for joining me on this journey. *Wyoming Mountain Murder* is the fourth book in my Cowboy State Lawmen series. I've had such great fun writing this series set in the beautiful state of Wyoming. Please forgive some of the liberties I have taken with the setting of Laramie and making it my own to enhance the story. As a veteran, I found it a pleasure developing strong characters who support and protect their community even though their jobs also put them in danger. I hope you enjoy Brian and Charlie's adventure since I wrote it for you.

I love chatting with readers and would welcome hearing your thoughts on this story. Let's stay in touch. If you're interested in learning more about this book, others that I've written or contacting me, go to my website: www.junorushdan.com.

My sincerest gratitude to you for being the reason I'm able to do what I love each day. Thank you for your support!

Juno Rushdan

WYOMING MOUNTAIN MURDER

—

Juno Rushdan

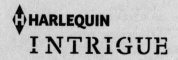

To the gung ho Rushdan tribe. You are my everything.

HARLEQUIN®
INTRIGUE™

Recycling programs for this product may not exist in your area.

ISBN-13: 978-1-335-58267-6

Wyoming Mountain Murder

Copyright © 2023 by Juno Rushdan

For questions and comments about the quality of this book, please contact us at CustomerService@Harlequin.com.

Harlequin Enterprises ULC
22 Adelaide St. West, 41st Floor
Toronto, Ontario M5H 4E3, Canada
www.Harlequin.com

Printed in U.S.A.

Juno Rushdan is a veteran US Air Force intelligence officer and award-winning author. Her books are action-packed and fast-paced. Critics from *Kirkus Reviews* and *Library Journal* have called her work "heart-pounding James Bond-ian adventure" that "will captivate lovers of romantic thrillers." For a free book, visit her website: www.junorushdan.com.

Books by Juno Rushdan

Harlequin Intrigue

Cowboy State Lawmen

Wyoming Winter Rescue
Wyoming Christmas Stalker
Wyoming Mountain Hostage
Wyoming Mountain Murder

Fugitive Heroes: Topaz Unit

Rogue Christmas Operation
Alaskan Christmas Escape
Disavowed in Wyoming
An Operative's Last Stand

A Hard Core Justice Thriller

Hostile Pursuit
Witness Security Breach
High-Priority Asset
Innocent Hostage
Unsuspecting Target

Tracing a Kidnapper

Visit the Author Profile page at Harlequin.com.

CAST OF CHARACTERS

Charlie Sharp—Tough as nails, she's the owner of the Underground Self-Defense school. She has a troubled past and a secret that could blow her life apart.

Brian Bradshaw—A former elite soldier, he's now an officer with the Laramie Police Department, assigned to a joint task force. He would do anything to help a friend.

Rocco Sharp—An ATF agent assigned to the joint task force, he's coworkers and friends with Brian and is Charlie's cousin.

Haley Olsen—A client at the Underground Self-Defense school.

Seth Olsen—A police officer at the LPD and Haley's husband.

Chapter One

"He's going to kill me."

Charlie Sharp recognized the panicked voice on the other end of the burner phone. It was a VIP client. A woman who not only took classes with her but also was in the process of using some of Charlie's *off-the-books* services.

"Slow down." Cradling her cell phone between her ear and shoulder, she turned the key in the dead bolt and finished locking up for the night. "Did he find out you're planning to leave him?" She adjusted the strap of her gym bag on her shoulder. "Tell me what happened."

Haley groaned, as if in agonizing pain.

A fist of tension gathered in Charlie's chest. She understood all too well the type of brutality her client—*her friend*—endured at the hands of her monstrous husband. Charlie tried not to get too close to any of the customers who came to Underground Self-Defense—USD—the school she'd built all on her own. There were hazards in getting emotionally attached, but she had a soft spot for survivors of domestic violence and invariably got sucked into their lives.

"Haley, talk to me."

"There's no time. He hurt me pretty bad." Haley sobbed over the line. "You have to help me." The terror in her voice was palpable, chilling Charlie's blood. "Oh, God, he's coming back."

The call disconnected.

For a moment, Charlie stared at the screen, thinking. Should she call Haley back? If her husband heard the phone ringing, would it only make him angrier?

The same applied for a text message.

Charlie hopped in her Dodge Hellcat, tossing her bag in the passenger's seat, and cranked the engine. Tearing out of the parking lot behind her USD school, she hit the side street, Garfield, and then at the stop sign made a right onto Third, the main road through town.

Once she cleared downtown, taking Highway 230, the Snowy Range Road, she gunned the accelerator, pushing the seven hundred horsepower supercharged V-8 of her leather-lined beast to the max.

Logic told her to call the police. That was what a reasonable person would do in a potentially life-threatening scenario.

But Charlie couldn't, for the same reason Haley had called her instead of the cops.

Haley's husband was a detective in the Laramie Police Department. His brothers in blue had protected him countless times. Looking the other way. Not filing reports. Her husband's threats had always coerced Haley not to press charges against him no matter how badly he'd beaten her. The cycle of abuse simply continued.

Drawing in a deep breath, Charlie struggled to suppress her own childhood memories. Of her mother's screams. The sight of her bruises. The endless excuses she had made to justify her husband's violent nature.

The first six years of her life, Charlie had grown up in a constant state of fear.

Fear of what would set off her father the next time. The television tuned to the wrong show. Dinner not ready on time. Meat loaf served when he had a craving for fried chicken. Back talk from her mother. Charlie playing with her dolls too loudly. Sometimes it was just the weather. Too hot. Too muggy. Too much snow.

Sometimes there wasn't any reason at all, except that her dad was a cruel man, who didn't need one.

On and on it went until the summer she turned seven.

That was when her life changed forever.

She cut left, taking the turn for the dirt road that led out to the Olsen ranch. The twenty acres had been divided between the two brothers. Seth had Ranch B, eight acres with a lake large enough for fishing. The other brother, Abel, who had Down syndrome, had gotten Ranch A, with more acreage and the pig farm.

The road forked. She took the right path, headed for Seth's place. Slowing down, she didn't want to give the impression that she had been driving like a bat out of hell or skid as she navigated the ruts of the gravel road. The dread that had been gnawing at her since Haley's desperate phone call took another bite.

Beyond the wrought-iron arches that had Olsen scrolled along the top, the modest house appeared in the moonlight. Charlie stared with apprehension at the small wooden cabin. It was so plain and simple. And *dark*. Haley's car, a white sedan, was parked in front of the attached garage. From the windows, nothing stirred inside the house.

Charlie brought her Dodge to a stop on the path before reaching the garage, far away from the house, and stuffed her cell phone in the pocket of her leggings.

Hopping out of the car, she hustled around to the trunk and popped it open. She fished around in the crate that she kept back there and found a flashlight. The big metal one, long and thick with hefty weight. In a pinch, she could use it as a weapon.

Closing the trunk, she scanned the area. There was nothing nearby. No other houses. No odd sounds. Only the trees swaying in the quiet, the croaking frogs and crickets, and the lake behind the house. She couldn't even make out Ranch A in the distance.

The night air smelled of dying lake grass and still water, and held the heat of the day.

A breeze stirred the birch limbs overhanging the house. As she approached the sagging wooden porch, there were no sounds coming from inside the cabin. No yelling. No crying.

Nothing but an eerie stillness. Goose bumps prickled her arms. She rubbed them away as she marched across the overgrown lawn.

Was Haley okay? Was Seth still there?

His car wasn't parked outside.

But why was the house so dark?

Something about this was off, wrong. So wrong. She crept up the rickety porch steps, each groan from the wood warning her to tread carefully. Floorboards creaked as she drew closer to the front door.

There was no bell on the jamb. She pulled open the screen door; hinges in need of WD-40 squeaked. With two knuckles, she rapped on the door, and it yawned open like someone hadn't closed it all the way for the latch to catch.

"Hello?" she called out.

No answer.

Haley could be unconscious, bleeding to death. Or worse. Seth was pond scum. Well, actually, he was lower than pond scum. He was the type who would leave his wife injured, alone, in desperate need of medical attention, and in the dark for sheer spite.

The type of man Charlie wouldn't spit on if he was on fire.

She nursed her anger to keep at bay the worry flitting around her belly like fireflies.

"Hello? Haley?" Every muscle tightened as she listened intently, straining to pick up the slightest whimper.

Still not a peep.

Forget about trespassing if it meant she could save a life. She stepped over the threshold, letting the screen door slam shut, and edged into the house.

With a sense of foreboding ballooning inside her, she slowly eased deeper, into the living room. She pressed the button on her flashlight, the sound of the click reassuring, but it didn't turn on. Shaking it, she hoped the problem was just a short and that the flashlight might at least flicker.

No luck. The batteries were dead. She usually changed them once a year. But there should be a new twelve pack of D cell alkaline batteries in the trunk.

She debated going back outside to change the ones that weren't working. But it was better to find Haley first. Every second counted in a life-or-death situation. It had taken Charlie twenty minutes to get there. No telling how much damage Seth had done to Haley in that amount of time. Broken bones? Swollen eyes? Internal bleeding? Concussion?

All good incentives to hurry.

The curtains were drawn back, letting in plenty of moonlight for her to see. She wanted to avoid touching light switches or much of anything if this turned out to be a worst-case scenario—a crime scene.

In the living room, a tired leather sofa faced a fireplace and flat-screen TV. Magazines covered the coffee table: everything from gossip rags, recipes, to *National Geographic*. An ashtray filled with cigarette butts sat on top of a *TV Guide*.

She stepped into a bedroom. Looked like the primary. A king-size bed with a blue-and-white quilt dominated the space, only leaving room for a couple of nightstands. On one of the bedside tables was a glass of water. Moving on, Charlie peeked her head into a cramped bathroom next door. The shower curtain was pulled back, revealing an empty tub. But something on the sink caught her eye.

Dark spots on the porcelain gleamed in the moonlight. She stepped inside and leaned over the sink for a closer look.

Blood.

Not much. Only a few drops. Maybe from a nosebleed. But it was enough to spur her on quickly throughout the rest of the house.

The dense, muggy air was thick as soup indoors thanks to the lack of air-conditioning.

She came to a second bedroom, similar to the first and also empty. From the hall, she entered the kitchen, coming up to the peninsula on the right side. The space was small and jam-packed, even with just the basics and a slim top freezer fridge.

But the back door was wide open.

She walked around the peninsula and halted.

A bright spill of moonlight, cutting through the kitchen, spotlighted a swath of something dark smeared on the floor all the way out through the back door. She stared at the grimy strip. It wasn't mud.

Glancing around the kitchen, she saw more. Splattered on the cabinets and wall.

Was it blood?

Panic welled up inside her. She edged closer to the trail on the floor, careful not to step in it. Squatting, she held up her phone, activated the light and illuminated the smear.

Oh, God. Definitely blood. Black. Sticky. And a lot of it. *Everywhere.*

Dizziness swept over her, like the wind had been knocked right out of her.

Regaining her equilibrium, she could only gape as the full import of what she saw registered. Then she was struck by a wave of horror. Outrage. Utter disbelief.

She swallowed with difficulty, tasting bile, struggling to regain control of her emotions.

"No," she whispered to herself. But her gaze swept across the kitchen, skated over the back porch, out to the grass.

It was true.

That was the kind of appalling trail left behind after dragging a bloody body.

Charlie wasn't sure if the blood led to the lake, where a corpse could've been weighted down in the water, or to the garage, where it could've been loaded into the trunk of a car and disposed of elsewhere.

She stood, and skirting the edge of the blood, went out onto the porch and headed toward the lake, to see if she could spot anything in the water. Not wanting to step in the evidence, she stayed clear of the possible path of blood.

Sweat dripped down her spine. Her stomach churned.

She dialed Haley's number and desperately hoped. Hoped that it hadn't been her body dragged out of the house. Hoped that the woman had finally gotten the upper hand on her abuser and killed him before he got to her first.

Charlie knew how to handle a situation like that. How to help Haley get through it.

The call went straight to voice mail.

The sliver of hope withered inside her, leaving a bitter taste in her mouth. Guilt clogged her throat.

What was she going to do?

Calling the police was a necessity. But it was also something she would not, could *not* do.

The boys in blue would use the good ole boy system and do whatever was possible to protect one of their own. Somehow the line of questioning would implicate Charlie instead of Seth. She was the one at the crime scene. Hell, she'd just contaminated it.

Then Charlie's off-the-books services would inevitably be discovered.

No. Calling the cops was out of the question.

So, she did the next best thing and dialed the one person in the world she trusted.

"Hello," Rocco Sharp answered.

Technically, he was her cousin, but they were as close as siblings and she loved him like a brother.

"I need help. I've got a problem."

"Make it quick. I'm working. Can't stay on the phone long."

As a Bureau of Alcohol, Tobacco, Firearms and Explosives agent assigned to a special joint task force in town, there was no telling what work entailed for him this evening because he couldn't discuss it.

"Haley Olsen called me. He was beating her again. I'm out at their place. I think Seth did something to her. Killed her."

"Sure you're not overreacting?" Rocco asked. "Look, I get that Haley, her situation, is a trigger for you."

Seeing any abused woman sparked Charlie's anger, and she wasn't unwilling to accept that she might be more sensitive to Haley's circumstances since it reminded her of her mother. Woman married to a violent cop who was protected by the force. Charlie had already lived through the nightmare once and knew how that story was going to end.

Maybe it already had.

"I'm not overreacting. It's dark inside the house," Charlie said. "And I found blood. Lots of blood. Like there was a body that was moved. No sign of Haley or Seth, but her car is still here. Her phone goes straight to voice mail."

Rocco swore. "You broke into the house?"

"The door was open."

More curses from him stung her ear. "This is bad."

Squeezing her eyes shut, she nodded to herself. "I know."

"You're always up to your neck in trouble," he said, and she didn't bother trying to deny it since it was true. "You've got to call 911."

"No way." She shook her head, a reflex even though he couldn't see her. "If you were here, I *might* consider it. Otherwise—"

"I can't come. I'm sort of stuck in a situation outside of Laramie." Rocco sighed. "But I can send someone else."

There was no one else she trusted. No one who would give her the benefit of the doubt. No one who would take her at her word. Not like Rocco. And he was out of town. "Who could you possibly send?"

"Someone who'd be on your side. That's what you need."

She groaned at the lack of a name. "I need to know."

"Bradshaw," he gritted out.

"What? Is this a sick joke?" Brian Bradshaw was one of them. "He's a cop." Which made him the last person she wanted getting involved. Better for her to hightail it out of there right now.

"He's a friend. With a badge. He can look out for you. Act as a buffer between you and the rest of the Laramie PD."

Technically, his friend was on loan from the police department, currently assigned to the same joint task force as her cousin. During the time they had worked together, she was painfully aware that the two guys had grown close. Hung out. Had dinner. Watched football games. She often teased Rocco about their bromance, but that did not mean she trusted their mutual acquaintance to protect her back.

Clutching the phone tighter, she hated the idea for more reasons than she was able to count. She would do anything to avoid that man.

Brian Bradshaw had an insidious way of staying so warm and upbeat, regardless of how icy and rude she was to him on purpose. His unflappable congeniality rankled her senseless. No one was that nice. All the time. He was hiding something behind his saccharine facade and annoyingly handsome face. One she admittedly enjoyed looking at too much. Even though no man would ever make her go weak in the knees or soft in the head, no matter how attractive he was.

But Brian was simply too much…of everything. Too talkative. Too ingratiating. Too persistent.

Not that any of it mattered because everything boiled down to one insurmountable fact.

He was a cop.

Just like her father.

It was bad enough her cousin was an ATF agent. Although she had grown up with Rocco, trusted him with her life, she even kept him at a distance. Never letting him get too close. She made sure that he didn't know anything about her illicit activities. He was smart enough not to ask her questions he didn't want answers to. The secrets she harbored remained off his radar. She planned on keeping it that way.

For her sake as well as his.

On the breeze, she caught a smell in the air. Her stomach flip-flopped as she put a name to the distinct scent.

Smoke.

Charlie spun around. Flames were visible through the windows of the house. Flickering. Spreading. Very, very, fast.

"The house…" She swallowed, staring in disbelief. "The house is on fire," she muttered, half to herself.

"What? I don't understand," he said, and neither did she. "Didn't you say the place was empty?"

Charlie started walking toward the cabin, mind scrambling to make sense of it, every nerve ending alight and crackling like a fuse.

This was the epitome of bad.

Another thought occurred to her. Somewhere in the darkness of the property was whoever set the fire.

A chill crawled under her skin. "I'm getting out of here. Got to go." She ended the call without another word and ran, heading for her car.

Charlie bolted across the lawn, and as she came around the side of the cabin, she caught sight of the three-hundred-gallon propane tank used to heat and power the place. Her mouth went dry as dust. She veered away from the combustible tank, sprinting faster, heart pumping double-time as adrenaline surged through her veins. But by then, it was too late.

The house exploded. The blast concussion hurled her off her feet. Heat seared the air. Singed her hair.

Her back slammed against the ground, her head hitting something even harder. Pain spiked through her.

And the world went dark.

Chapter Two

"Will you help Charlie get to the bottom of things while keeping her out of trouble with your guys?" Rocco asked, referring to the police department.

"Are you sure you really want me on this, bearing in mind what I just told you?" Brian would understand if Rocco reconsidered, but it was important for him to know. "You can get someone else. Maybe Nash."

Nash Garner was the FBI lead and supervisory special agent of their task force. The guy could be a bit brusque and taciturn, but he was fair. Too bad Becca, the other agent on their team, was on vacation.

"I'm sure. It needs to be you." There was no hesitation in Rocco's voice, which was encouraging. "I think you're the only one who can get it done, even if it means a delicate balancing act on your part. Just don't tell Charlie what you told me. She'll panic if you do. Take care of her for me, won't you?"

"Yeah, all right," Brian said, realizing he had just made a promise that was going to be nearly impossible to keep.

The second he hung up the phone, he wondered what he was about to get himself involved in.

A sliver of unease wormed in his gut.

Helping out a buddy and coworker didn't require a second thought. Much less asking too many questions. He was tight with Rocco, but this situation was tricky. Especially when it came to Charlie.

The woman was an enigma wrapped in ice. He longed to chip away at her permafrost. No matter how long it took. He estimated it was going to take a while because Charlie was cold, cold, cold. Completely unattainable. On every level unavailable.

Not that it deterred him from wanting to make Charlie his one day.

What could he say?

He enjoyed a *challenge*. That single word summed her up perfectly.

Last year, Rocco had been added to the special joint task force and had moved to Laramie. That was how Brian had met Charlie. Funny, she'd been living there for years, and before then their paths had never crossed. Almost as though she hadn't existed. But once he had seen her, been introduced, it was like he kept getting sucked into her orbit. Running into her everywhere. His thoughts always veering back to her.

Charlie on the other hand wanted nothing to do with him. You would've thought he had the bubonic plague the way she steered clear of him. Every one of his attempts to get to know her she had stymied, despite his best efforts. His offer to teach self-defense classes at her school for free, to take care of a plumbing issue at her house—once again, no strings attached, to fix her flat tire when he'd once seen her broken down on the road, to buy her a cup of coffee, had all been met with stone-cold rejection.

When they'd bumped into each other at a charity gala for a women's shelter in Cheyenne—both without dates—he'd sworn it had been fate. That things between them might change that night. For a couple of perfect hours, it had. The evening felt like the beginning of something.

Then she'd gone back to barely speaking to him while he couldn't stop thinking about her.

It was maddening.

Doing this favor for Rocco might be the key to getting closer to her.

Or it could be the biggest mistake that he ended up regretting.

Either way, this was going to be problematic. He'd already explained the potential complications to Rocco. Nonetheless, his friend trusted his judgment and had given him the green light to assist since Rocco was busy out of town, doing some undercover work.

Brian set down his first beer that he'd been nursing outside on his porch while enjoying the balmy summer air, stargazing. Wyoming in general, but specifically, out here in the countryside, boasted some of the darkest skies. An ideal spot for spying constellations. Even the Milky Way.

Great for clearing his head, restoring his soul.

Fortunately, he wasn't too far from the Olsen

place. Or Charlie's. About ten minutes to each, but in different directions. Seemed as though folks who lived out on the outskirts of town, close to the mountains, liked their space. Made sense to swing by the Olsen ranch first, take a look. Then he'd check on Charlie and have a chat.

Pushing his concerns aside, he grabbed his badge, his gun, clipping the holster to his belt, hopped in his truck and drove off. He took out his cell and dialed dispatch over at the Laramie PD.

"Hey, this Detective Brian Bradshaw. I received a report about a fire at Detective Seth Olsen's place over on—"

"Already got it, Bradshaw. Seth's brother phoned in something about hearing a huge boom. Then he saw a fire."

His gut tightened. "There was an explosion?"

"Apparently."

Things had gone from horrible to worse faster than he had expected.

"Station twenty-four is there now putting out the fire," the dispatch said.

Brian did a quick calculation in his head, factoring in the location of the fire station from the ranch. "How did they get there so fast?"

"They were already in the area responding to another incident. The one over at the Olsen ranch took priority, with the explosion and fire."

Brian peered through the windshield in the direction of the ranch. Smoke billowed in the night sky.

The scent was carried on a breeze through his rolled down window.

Charlie. "Were any bodies found on-site? Anyone injured?"

"No casualties yet," the dispatch said, and *yet* echoed in Brian's head. "They've requested canines to go through the place and look for remains once the fire is out."

"Any idea what caused the fire or the explosion?"

"Haven't heard. The new fire marshal is out there, too. I'm sure he'll report back soon as he's had a chance to properly investigate."

Brian had heard a new guy had taken over the position. "What's the name?"

"Powell. Sawyer Powell."

He wondered if he was related to Holden Powell, the chief deputy of the sheriff's department. "Okay. Thanks." He disconnected.

Change of plans. Slowing down, Brian made a U-turn and headed toward Charlie's house instead. No one was found at the scene out at Seth's. Investigators had the situation in hand. There was nothing for him to do at the ranch now besides get in the way. Not to mention that his presence would only have others questioning why he was there.

Finding Charlie and getting details firsthand was the best way for him to start.

She was only a couple of miles away. He'd had no idea that she lived so close to him until the day he'd spotted her on this road with a flat tire. Meaner than a rattlesnake, she had made it crystal clear that she didn't need his or anyone else's help. End of discussion.

Hopefully there had been a tectonic shift in her perspective in that respect since then.

It only took Brian a few minutes until he pulled into her driveway alongside her Hellcat. Nothing sexier than a strong, beautiful woman behind the wheel of a sleek muscle car. Even the color suited her. Frostbite blue.

She didn't have much land. About an acre and a half, maybe two. Neighbors had plenty of breathing room, not on top of another. The house was set close to the road, which he didn't care for, with most of the land behind it.

Grabbing his cowboy hat, he climbed out of his truck. He smoothed his hair back before putting on his Stetson. As he passed her car, a twinge of jealousy zipped through him over all that speed and torque. But nothing offered a better view of the road or more rugged protection than his F150.

He strode up to her porch, wondering what kind of reception he'd receive. Cold or lukewarm?

Brian hoped for the latter. For once.

The curtain in the front window closest to the door was yanked aside. Charlie appeared. She glared at him, shook her head as if exasperated, and stormed away.

The welcome was going to be icy.

As usual. *No big surprise there.*

Footsteps pounded inside, drawing closer. The door flew open. Charlie put a fist on her lean hip, cocked her head, and up went those eyebrows. He met her striking green eyes, a volatile color he could never forget no matter how hard he tried. As he drank in the sight of her, it was as if the world dropped out from under him.

The woman took his breath away every time he saw her.

Although she and Rocco were cousins, they were remarkably different. Rocco was big and imposing, with dark hair and brown skin thanks to his native Hawaiian heritage on his father's side. While Charlie had a creamy porcelain complexion, white-blond hair, and a slender yet athletic figure, though she still managed to be equally intimidating. Her personality was a force of nature.

But tonight, she looked as though she'd been the one put through the wringer. His gaze slid over her disheveled hair, which had grass and splinters of wood in it, down her mud-spattered T-shirt and dirty leggings, but then whipped back up to the fresh scrapes on her arms and chin.

"You're bleeding." He reached out to touch her face.

Charlie slapped his hand away and stroked the spot he was referring to. She glanced at the drops of blood on her fingertips. "It's nothing." Straightening, she looked back up at him. Even though she was five-nine, he still had a good four inches on her. "I told Rocco that *you* were the last person on earth I wanted him to call."

Brian let the sharp-tongued remark roll off his back. Something he was good at. Most survivors were.

He gripped the brim of his Stetson and tipped his hat at her. "Nice to see you, too." Undeterred by her thick veneer of cool disdain, he mustered a smile, determined to kill her with kindness. "May I come in? It would be better to discuss things inside, ma'am."

Her scowl faltered as she rocked back on her heels. "Don't ma'am me. I'm not a gazillion years old. I've told you before it rubs me the wrong way."

"I assure you that is not my intent. But if you want to tell me how to rub you the right way, I'm all ears." Her eyes narrowed to slits at that, and he thought it best to fill in the awkward silence before she slammed the door in his face. "My use of *ma'am* and *sir* is an old military habit that's hard to break. My apologies."

"You're prior service, huh." Her face softened, a little. "What branch? What did you do?"

"Army. Intelligence Support Activity. A Special Operations unit."

"Were you Special Ops or did you support them?"

"Both." It was hard to explain to civilians, but from the skeptical grimace on her face, he needed to try. "My old unit and our counterparts, SEAL Team Six, Delta Force are all considered Tier 1. You don't hear about ISA in the news, and they don't make movies about *The Activity*," he said, as they were often called, "but if not for us, Delta and DEVGRU— the SEALs—would have a tough time being successful." That was pretty much it in a simplified nutshell.

"Why did you quit Spec Ops to become a cop?" she asked, making *cop* sound like a dirty word.

He thought he was the one who was supposed to be asking the questions. Was she screening him to see if he was fit to assist? "This really isn't relevant."

"It is to me." She folded her arms across her chest. "You don't step foot across the threshold until I get an answer that satisfies me."

Brian tamped down the sigh rising in his chest. "My dad got sick. My mom couldn't handle the ranch on her own and couldn't afford to hire someone. So, I chose to stop doing something that I loved." He was no quitter. "To help the ones that I love. Joining the force was the closest fit for my skill set. But two years after I came back here, my father suffered a massive stroke. I had to put him into the Silver Springs Senior Living center. My mother couldn't bear to be away from him and moved in there also."

He'd given up his career for nothing. His specialized skills were going to waste. In the end, he had to sell the horses to pay for the exorbitant fees at the special care facility for both his parents.

Now, he was stuck. Back home. In Wyoming. As a cop. Living alone on land that he had no idea what to do with. Only thing stopping him from selling that, too, was his promise to his parents that he would hang on to the Bradshaw legacy.

The one good thing to come out of it was getting assigned to the joint task force.

"Satisfied?" he asked. This time when he smiled,

he didn't try to hide the sadness behind it. Not just for himself, but also for his father's tragic decline.

At least his parents were together. To this day, they made him believe in true love. Not in finding a soulmate, which he doubted was real, but in connecting with someone who understood you, whose faults you could tolerate if not appreciate, who brought light into the other's darkness, and vice versa.

"Not entirely, but enough," Charlie said, after a long moment. She stepped aside, letting him in. "How long have you been a *cop*?" Once again, contempt laced the word.

"Four years." The short period of time made him sound green, which he wasn't. She wouldn't be dealing with a patrol officer. "But I was fast-tracked to detective two years ago because of my military background."

She frowned when he'd thought she would find that reassuring. Obviously, he was missing something important.

"Let's get one thing straight," she said, shutting the door. "Just because Rocco trusts you doesn't mean that I do. Got it?"

Man, she was tough.

One more reason to like her.

"Fair enough." He removed his hat. "But you need to remember that I come in peace. To help you. In any way that I can."

"We'll see about that."

Stepping deeper into her home, he looked around. Minimalist, utilitarian furniture. Plain white walls. A few abstract pieces of art that provided hints of color. No knickknacks. No personal photos. A flat-screen TV sat on an empty bookcase opposite a taupe sofa. The coffee table was nothing more than a scratched metal storage trunk. Unopened cardboard boxes lined the far wall.

Since she'd gotten a flat tire on the road nearby almost nine months ago, he knew she hadn't just moved in. "How long have you lived here?"

"Two and half years."

It was as if the place was merely functional. A place to eat and sleep. Not a sanctuary. She hadn't even fully unpacked.

"You don't spend much time here, do you?" he asked.

"No. The USD is open seven days a week, fifteen hours a day to give anyone interested in taking a class a chance to fit one into their schedule." Glancing around, she stiffened. "Why do you ask?"

Not one to lie and not willing to get sidetracked by offending her, he said, "How about we get your face and arms cleaned up."

Charlie shook her head. "It's only a few cuts and some singed hair," she said, fingering a bunch of strands. "It can wait. Have a seat." She gestured to the living room.

She dropped into a chair across from the sofa. Beside her was an end table. On top of it was a lamp and a glass with amber liquid. He noted a hole in her leggings that exposed pale skin on her calf and blood.

Tending to her wounds, no matter how minor,

should be the priority, but he also sensed this needed to be on her terms. "It's going to be hard for me to focus with you injured and bleeding. Let's compromise. We get you bandaged up while you explain why I'm here. You do know how to compromise, don't you?" He was half joking. The other part of him wondered just how stubborn she really was.

A groan, fraught with impatience, rolled from Charlie. "I do." Her jaw clenched. "I simply don't do it often. There's generally no need."

Since he was making headway, he figured he'd push a bit further. "Where's your first-aid kit?"

Gripping the arms of the chair, she started to rise.

"Allow me to get it for you." He dared put a hand on her shoulder, urging her stay seated.

She flinched from his touch like his palm had scalded her. "I'm not an invalid."

"Clearly, but Rocco made me promise to take care of you."

"I don't think he meant like this."

No, he hadn't. "Still, he'd be happy if I did, and it'll earn me some brownie points with my mom." Hopefully with Charlie as well.

"I can't believe you care about brownie points with your mother." She looked him over, from head to toe and back up to his face. "Then again, I take it back. I can."

Why did that not sound like a compliment?

"Were you a Boy Scout, too?" she asked.

"As a matter of fact, I was. Cub Scout first." He left out the part about the Cubs being the equivalent of the Brownies where the term brownie point originated.

Charlie rolled her eyes. "Oh, give me a break."

How was that a bad thing?

She was a hard case. Only intensified the itch he would one day scratch.

He was an eternal optimist if nothing else. "Where's your first-aid stuff?"

"Lower kitchen cabinet, next to the pantry. Don't expect to find some fancy, tricked out med bag like you probably have."

With a curt nod, he went to grab it. In the cabinet, there were basic supplies that paled in comparison to what he had in his truck, much less in his house. At home, he had a complete suture kit. She didn't even have hydrogen peroxide or alcohol.

Not that it was necessary. The saline solution and antibiotic ointment would suffice. He also grabbed gauze along with bandages and paper towels.

He returned to the living room and knelt in front of her.

"No comment?" she asked, eyeing the supplies in his hands.

"You've got the essentials." Brian shrugged. "What's there to say?" He imagined her pantry and freezer to be the same. Basics only.

He tugged up her pant leg past her knee.

She grimaced. "Ouch."

Peering closer, he spotted what caused the pain. He yanked out a rather large fragment of wood embedded in her calf. Blood spurted from the wound.

He pressed a paper towel to it first. With the saline solution, he flushed the cut, eliciting a hiss of pain from her.

Wincing, she clutched his shoulder.

He poured a bit more solution on the deep gash.

Her grip on him tightened, and she swore. "Sorry. I'm not usually such a big baby."

"No problem." He dabbed at the wound with gauze, pleased the bleeding slowed. "Feel free to grab on to me anytime."

She glanced down at her hand on his shoulder. Her eyes flared wide as though she hadn't realized she was touching him. Pulling away, she grabbed the glass on the end table and took a healthy sip.

"What's your poison?" he asked, applying antibiotic ointment.

"Scotch. Twenty-one-year-old Glenfiddich."

Two things she splurged on, her car and her Scotch. It certainly wasn't her home decor.

He put a bandage on the cut. "At that price point, I bet it's pretty smooth. I'm more of a beer drinker myself."

"Of course, you are," she said with a slight sneer.

"What's that supposed to mean?" While he waited for a response, he cleaned the cut on her wrist above her smartwatch.

"It's the quintessential alcoholic beverage of the USA."

"And?"

Lowering her gaze, she shook her head as though she wasn't going to say anything else. But she did.

"It's very on brand for you." She looked at him. "Fits with your whole Captain America vibe."

That was nicest thing anyone had ever said to him. At the same time—she had hurled the words at him, sharp, little stones not intended to flatter—it was also the meanest.

Good thing he didn't have a big ego, but it was better she thought of him as a capable superhero than a dimwitted Dudley Do-Right.

If he searched hard enough, there was always a silver lining.

Rocco had once admitted that although he was the closest person to Charlie, they weren't exactly close. By her choice.

In that moment, Brian understood why she was alone. Why she had no pictures of family or friends hanging on the walls. It was because she had a knack for pushing people away. The sort of talent that was bred from pain. Or fear.

Perhaps both.

"You'll come to learn that my brand is more along the lines of Timex," he said, dabbing gauze saturated in saline solution on the cut on her chin. "I take a licking and keep on ticking." He winked.

Give it your best shot, Charlie.

She stared at him with an inscrutable expression on her face. Up close, she was even prettier. Mesmerizing eyes. The sultriest mouth. He tried hard not to think how her chin-length hair would feel tickling his bare chest. Then he tried even harder not to think about her lips doing the same thing.

With a gentle fingertip, he applied some ointment on her chin. She let out a shaky breath, her lips parting at contact. His pulse raced. His blood pumped hard through his veins as he took her in. The scent of her making its way deep into his lungs. Feminine musk, grass and smoke. Something passed between them, hot and intangible.

All too soon, she leaned back, pulling her face from his fingers.

Needing to get it together around her, he got up from the floor and sat in the chair on the other side of the end table. "Tell me the reason you called Rocco, and why you were at the Olsen ranch."

"First, you have to agree not to haul me in as a witness."

"Depends on what you tell me."

"Either you agree that this stays between us for now, off the record, or I have nothing else to say."

Brian had made a promise to Rocco, and going into this, he knew Charlie wouldn't make things easy. "I'm capable of coloring outside the lines, but I won't aid and abet."

Resting an elbow on her thigh, she pressed the heel of her palm to her forehead and stared down at her muddy sneakers. "I guess this is harder, repeating everything to you than it was telling my cousin."

Totally understandable. Normal even. "But I need to hear it from you."

"To see if I'm lying?" Those green eyes flashed up at him.

"When you play a game of whisper down the lane

or telephone, details in the message tend to get lost."
As a former human intelligence officer, getting information from people was his specialty. Firsthand was always best.

To weed out the lies.

To dig deeper to the truth.

To read between the lines of what they didn't want you to know.

"I was locking up USD when Haley called me." Tension was evident in the stiffness of her neck and bone-white knuckles of her clasped hands. "She told me that Seth was going to kill her. He was beating her again."

Frowning, Brian scooted to the edge of his seat. This was precisely what he wanted to avoid. A game of whispers. "What were her exact words?"

"He's going to kill me. He hurt me. It's bad." She made a noncommittal gesture as if she wasn't completely certain. "Then she asked me to come help her."

"She said *he*, not Seth?"

"Yeah, so what?"

There were rumors that Haley was unfaithful. The same applied to Seth. If true, they were both cheaters. "It's possible she was referring to a third party. Maybe a lover."

"At her house? Beating her?" Charlie yanked down her pant leg and jumped to her feet. "She never mentioned having a lover to me."

Most cheaters didn't go around bragging. "Doesn't mean it isn't possible." He wouldn't sugarcoat this.

"What I don't understand," he said, standing and striding closer to her, "is why Haley would call you instead of the police."

"Calling the cops was useless. The lot of you stick together." She waved an accusatory hand in his direction. "The one time she dialed 911, he had coerced her to say that she fell to explain her injuries. After those boys in blue left, he made her regret it. Most of the abuse was psychological, but not always. Many times, he left bruises and scars that I saw myself."

Brian's mind reeled. He had always considered Seth to be a good guy. Not an abusive jerk. Hell, Seth was not only a fellow cop, but they played tackle football together with some other guys on the force. Hung out from time to time afterward, having a few beers. Occasionally dinner. They weren't quite friends, like he was with Rocco, but they were certainly chummy.

All things he had shared with Rocco in full disclosure. Things his buddy thought best not to tell Charlie.

"That still doesn't explain why you," he stated. "Surely she has family or friends. Why did Haley Olsen call you?"

No way they were BFFs. Charlie wasn't the type to have a best friend. She was a lone wolf. Tortured and forbidding. All he wanted to do was get her to stop running. To show her that she didn't have do it all on her own. To chase the shadows from her gaze.

Could he?

She picked up her drink, took a swig and gave a one-shouldered shrug. "I don't know."

He stepped toward her. "I think you do."

A beat. A second's hesitation. She blinked before looking away and setting her glass down with a *clink*. "I don't. She shared a lot with me during training sessions at USD. It's good to vent while you're sweating. Maybe she felt that she could trust me to help her."

"What would instill that degree of trust? To ask you to intervene with her husband?"

She nipped her bottom lip. A subtle gesture, but a telling one. At best, she was hiding something. At worst, she was lying.

Damn it.

He shook his head. She had no idea who she was dealing with. His gaze dropped back to her mouth. Those rosy-pink lips pursed in a way that made him imagine she was holding back an avalanche of secrets. Made him want to kiss those secrets right out of her. Slowly. One by one.

A technique he had never employed before. His specialty as a human intelligence officer had been uncovering the truths others sought to bury. He'd been extremely proficient at his job, doing whatever was necessary. Some skills were never lost. He might be rusty, but it was like riding a bike.

He'd find out what she didn't want him to know. Once he was on to something, he was like a bloodhound that didn't stop. "If something has happened to Haley," he said, still not entirely certain that something had, "the police will come to question you once they check her phone records."

"The cell phone is a burner I gave her so she could communicate without Seth knowing. The number I gave her to contact me is to my own burner. The cops won't be able to trace it back to me."

A vehicle tore up to the house. The dull sound of tires spitting through the lawn drew their gazes to the front window.

"Are you expecting someone?" he asked.

She shook her head. "No."

Years of ingrained training had him grasping the hilt of his weapon. He inched over a step and looked through the window. High beams were focused on the house, like a spotlight, blinding him.

Next thing he knew, there were gunshots.

Chapter Three

Charlie reached for Brian, to get him away from the window. Out of the line of fire.

But he was already in motion, lunging for her with startling speed. He grabbed hold of her, taking her down to the floor, his body covering hers.

Pop, pop, pop, pop. Four more rounds blew out her bay window. Shattered glass rained down. A lamp exploded. Bullets bit into the walls.

An engine revved, tires spun outside and peeled away.

Heart pounding violently, she lay there, frozen for a minute. Even if she had wanted to move, it would have been impossible. His solid, heavy body had her pinned to the floor.

Slowly, he uncurled the strong arm he had wrapped around her head. He stared down at her, his warm chocolate-brown gaze caressing her face as lean, masculine muscle brushed against her. An electric jolt ripped through her that had nothing to do with their close call with death and everything to do with him.

You're just confusing the rush of adrenaline with something else.

That's what she tried to tell herself anyway. "They're gone." Her voice was a whisper she didn't recognize. "You can get off me now."

When he didn't immediately move, she pressed her palms to his chest to shove him away and instantly regretted it. Hard, taut muscle shifted beneath her fingers. The ridges and valleys teasing her, tempting her. His warmth penetrated through clothes and skin, deep into her bones. The weight of his body was so comforting that she couldn't bring herself to push him off.

"I just wanted to make sure they didn't swing back around for another try," he said, his soft breath grazing her cheek.

"Oh." She hadn't considered that possibility.

He cradled her face with a tenderness that had her throat growing tight and her heart drumming harder.

Part of her couldn't wait for him to move. The other part wanted to cling to him a little longer, holding him close, soaking up his heat. Even the scent of him was sunshine and happiness and sexy sweat. He smelled better than anyone she'd ever met.

She struggled to catalog the terror tangling with the thrill that stung the insides of her veins as she found herself slipping into a strange passivity trapped beneath him.

God, she hated the effect he had on her.

"Think it's safe now?" she asked in a hushed voice.

"Yeah, I think so." He gave a little nod, his mouth

a hairbreadth from hers. "But stay down and let me check to be sure." Rolling off her, he pushed to a crouch with his sidearm in his hand.

The chill that swept over Charlie in the absence of his body heat made her shiver. She glanced at the shattered glass, holes in the wall and the mess left behind from the bullets meant for her.

Brain crept to the window, pressed his back against the wall and craned his neck around the sill. A moment later, he said, "All clear. It's safe to get up." He strode back over to her and offered his hand.

But she couldn't take it, actually more afraid of what might happen, of how she might feel if she touched him again, than of the shooter coming back.

She got up on her own. "Thanks. You're quick on your feet."

"Any idea who was shooting at you? Or why?"

"No." The only thing she could think was that it was somehow related to whatever had happened to Haley. "Maybe it was Seth."

A frown tugged between his dark brows. "Why would a cop drive by your house and shoot at you?" he asked, sounding as though it was outside the realm of possibility.

"Cops commit crimes, too. Premeditated. Out of passion. Desperation. Don't look at me as if I'm delusional."

Jaw hardening, he rubbed the back of his neck. "You're right. Some cops are bad. But not most. I would know."

"Maybe you don't see too clearly with the rose-colored glasses you wear."

"I've been through the carnage of war, endured physical nightmares that would traumatize most and seen how ugly humanity can be. Trust and believe, I see clearly." He took a deep breath. The corners of his mouth lifted in a soft smile. He raised his palms, like a white flag, suggesting peace. "Let's not get sidetracked. I get you've made being mean your hobby, but it's not going to get you answers or help Haley. How about a truce since we're on the same side. What do you say?"

She took a step back. Something inside her deflated, all the anger and annoyance fizzling away at that one little benign act. Perhaps what made it so powerful was that it seemed sincere.

This man kept throwing her off-kilter, softening her despite her efforts to maintain her hardened edge. Part of her regretted giving him a hard time. The other part remembered he was a cop.

Snap out of it. He was probably just trying to get her to lower her guard. No one was ever that nice. At least not to her.

Being mean wasn't a hobby. It was a defense mechanism. The best one she had, but she couldn't ignore that working together was the only way to get answers. "Okay, truce."

"What motive would Seth have for coming here? Why would he shoot at you?"

"Because I know what he did. I saw the blood in the house. Then someone set a fire and the whole place went up. Someone set it on fire deliberately. He'd shoot at me because I'm a witness."

"You fled a crime scene?"

"Don't say it like that, as if I'm the one who committed the crime. I'm not. I was only trying to help a friend. Then I panicked."

"First, I'm going to call in this shooting," he said, and she opened her mouth to protest. "A report has to be filed about this. It's nonnegotiable. Then you're going to walk me through exactly what happened after you spoke to Haley tonight."

Gritting her teeth, she relented with a nod. "But I don't want the report filed with the Laramie PD. If you've got to call this in, do it with the sheriff's office. Deal?"

One LPD officer in her home and another possibly shooting at her was more than enough. She didn't want to involve any more.

"I can live with that."

CHARLIE RELIVED THE details of the evening for Brian, enduring his relentless barrage of questions as he tried to pick apart her story.

"Then the cabin exploded. I was knocked out for a minute or two from the blast. When I came to, I left." There had been fiery debris everywhere. Strewn across the yard. Covering Haley's car. She was lucky to be alive.

"You didn't actually witness anything other than arson," he finally said, standing beside her in the kitchen.

"What about all of the blood in the house?" She took another sip of scotch from her freshly poured glass. This was her *only drink in case of emergency or celebration* bottle of Glenfiddich. The night called for two more fingers worth. "I'm telling you it's from a dead body. Haley's."

"But you didn't see a body, did you?" he asked.

"No, but Haley's missing. She's not answering her phone and her car was at the house. It was blown up in the explosion."

"Maybe she got the drop on her husband. Did something to him. Used his car to transport the body. Then set the fire."

"Seth Olsen is no featherweight. Haley is a hundred and twenty soaking wet. Seth's got to weigh at least as much as you." She estimated two hundred pounds of muscle easy. "She couldn't have disposed of a body on her own. Why would she even try, knowing that I was on the way?"

Straightening, he narrowed his eyes, studying her suddenly with a measured glance.

She had tipped her hand, said the wrong thing. But what?

"You're the *friend* someone calls when they need to get rid of a body. That's why she dialed your number and no one else." It was a statement. Not a question.

No, no. He was not going to turn this around on her, making her a suspect.

She swore under her breath, wanting to curse her cousin for sending Brian. "Haley hadn't been plotting to kill her husband. She'd been planning to leave him. I think Seth might've found out and that was the reason he beat her tonight. I honestly don't know why she called me. Other than she must've known I'd come regardless of the risks to myself. For the record, I've never helped anyone get rid of a body." But there was always a first time for everything.

Brian seemed to mull that over while assessing her. "Let's stop speculating. The police will be looking for Haley and Seth. One or both will turn up. No casualties were reported at the house. I'll know for certain once the canines go through the debris. The cadaver dogs will pick up whatever is left of any blood."

"Someone started the fire," she insisted. "Deliberately. To cover up what I saw in there." That same person was also probably the one who had shot at her. Well, they had messed with the wrong woman. Because now she wasn't just scared and appalled. She was angry.

"I'm not doubting it."

"You only doubt that Seth was responsible."

"I didn't say that." Brian sighed. "Look, jumping to conclusions is counterproductive. It'll get us nowhere. I prefer to investigate and let the evidence speak for itself."

A car pulled up outside with red and blue flashing lights. No siren wailing.

"I'm not going to say anything about Haley's phone call," she said, "or about going to the ranch."

His brow furrowed. "You have to."

"No. I don't. I only agreed to let you report the shooting."

"You were at a crime scene. You need to give an official statement."

"I will. After we find evidence. Discreetly." There was a knock at the door. "Let's see if I can trust you." She doubted it. "Play this my way. Got it?"

"This isn't a game."

"I know." It was a gamble.

She answered the door.

"I'm Chief Deputy Holden Powell. I take it your lack of a front window is from the shots fired?"

"Yes. Please, come in." She opened the door wider for him.

The deputy stepped inside.

"Holden." Brian strode over and extended his hand.

The two men shook. "I was surprised to hear from you tonight, Brian."

"Unfortunate circumstances made it necessary."

"How many shots were fired?" the deputy asked.

Charlie closed the door. "Five."

"Did either of you see who it was?" Holden looked between them.

They both shook their heads.

"No. The shooter sped off," Brian added. "I thought it best not to pursue. I wanted to make sure Charlie was all right. Also, in case there was more than one, perhaps a second shooter on foot meant to finish the job."

Another terrifying notion that hadn't occurred to her. Then again, she hadn't expected anyone to shoot at her in her home. With her side business, she sometimes encountered people who wanted to do her harm. It was usually up close and personal. But she could handle herself in a physical altercation. This attempt to hurt her by taking cowardly potshots was something else.

"Did you happen to see the make or the model or color of the vehicle?"

Another shake of the head from Brian and her.

"Any idea who might want to kill you?" the deputy asked. "Or why?"

Brian fixed her with a stare. One that pleaded with her to do what he thought was the right thing. She tensed under the intensity of his gaze, but she wasn't changing her mind.

She needed his cooperation. Not his judgment. "I've made a few enemies in town, but I can't say with certainty who might've done this or why." She glanced at Brian.

Could she count on him to keep his mouth shut?

Or would he disappoint her as so many others in her life had?

Folding his arms, he stayed silent, laser-focused on her, with disapproval he couldn't quite hide beneath his careful lack of expression.

To her amazement, there was no breach of trust.

The deputy walked through her living room, looking around. He put on gloves, pulled out an evidence bag and tweezers. "The good news is," he said, pulling out a shell casing embedded in the wall, "I didn't spot anyone watching the house like they planned to try again tonight." He dropped it in the evidence bag and plucked another from a different hole. "Still, it would best to keep your guard up."

She nodded in full agreement. "I plan to."

"You shouldn't stay the night here," Brian said.

The deputy clucked his tongue. "I have to agree. Best to sleep somewhere safer until we can figure out what's going on. Who's targeting you and why."

"First of all, there's no way I'm letting anyone run me out of my house. Besides, I've got nowhere else to go." She was ashamed to admit it, but it was the truth.

"Crash at Rocco's," Brian said. "He won't be back for a couple of days, and I've got a spare key to his place if you don't."

She was his cousin and didn't have a key. But his buddy did. How embarrassing. Not that she had given Rocco one to her house.

Still, it irked her.

"Or you could stay with me," Brian added. "I've got a comfy guest room."

The offer was generous. Even sweet. Suspiciously so, considering he assumed she had a hobby of being mean. Nobody was that nice to someone who was acting downright awful. The man was too good to be true. There was something wrong with him. Other than the fact that he was a cop. She just couldn't put her finger on it yet, but whatever *it* was would come back to bite her if she wasn't careful.

"I'll be fine here." She glanced over the hot mess of her living room. "Once I put some boards up on the window and clean up."

"I can help you with that," Brian said.

"No need. I'll take care of it."

Brian turned to the deputy. "Can you have forensics come out to take prints of the tire tracks out in the yard?"

"Sure, no problem." Holden nodded. "Won't do you much good until you have a suspect."

Brian slid her a knowing glance. "Yeah. Hopefully, we'll get one."

"Well, I'll leave you to it." The deputy headed for the door.

"One more thing," Brian said. "Is Sawyer Powell, the new fire marshal, any relation to you?"

"He's my brother. Why?"

"I heard there was a fire and subsequent explosion over at the Olsen ranch and that he's the one investigating. I plan to speak with him tomorrow."

"There's nobody better to have on the job than Sawyer."

"Glad to hear it." Brian shook his hand one more time. "Thanks again."

"No problem. I'll show myself out."

Once the chief deputy was gone, Charlie trudged back to the kitchen. Staring at the wide opening in her home, left by the shattered window, she took another gulp of scotch. Too bad she didn't have any spare wood boards to put up. But she wasn't handy and didn't tackle home projects often.

"I've got some extra plywood at home that I don't need," Brian said, as though reading her mind, coming up alongside her.

She set her glass down with a sad chuckle. "Of course, you do."

"Next, you're going to tell me you don't need it."

Mind reader indeed. "Of course, I am."

"Why?"

The question was so simple. A single word. Yet so hard to answer. She tipped her head back and met his curious gaze. "Force of habit." She shrugged. "It's safer to rely only on myself."

That way she wouldn't be disappointed when someone let her down. She never tested things with Rocco or his parents. They were the only family she had left. She didn't want to risk losing them, too, if they'd failed her in some way. Instead, she accepted the love and kindness they'd given and never asked for anything else.

"Not asking for help isn't strength, Charlie."

There was something sexy about the way her name rolled off his tongue. She realized she was staring and had to pull her gaze from his mouth.

"It's time to form new habits," he continued. "As you pointed out earlier, you're not old. You're capable of learning some new tricks."

At thirty, she was a far cry from old. More than capable of change, if she wanted to. She wasn't weak either. She had called Rocco for help, hadn't she?

But she didn't bother to highlight that since she also saw Brian's point.

The fact was he didn't know her, or understand what she had witnessed as a child, what she had survived.

The walls she put up around herself did keep others from getting in, but sometimes they were the only thing holding her together. It was about self-preservation. Not isolation.

"Your brand is Captain America," she said. "Not Dr. Phil *come sit on my sofa.*"

He grinned, and her pulse stuttered. "I'd love to get you on my sofa sometime," he said, his voice smooth and deep, making that flutter inside her dip lower. Dropping his gaze, he cleared his throat. "For now, I'm going to run home, grab the plywood and patch up your window while you get started cleaning. And for the sake of clarity, I'm not doing it for you. It's only out of a sense of obligation to Rocco. Captain America keeps his promises." He winked again.

It was so damn sexy, she struggled to come up with a witty retort, some snide remark that usually came to her as naturally as breathing.

"Do you have a gun?" he asked.

"Locked up in my safe." There were times when she needed one but preferred not to always carry it.

"Good. Get it. Keep it with you while I'm gone. I won't be long."

Brian grabbed his cowboy hat, and then he was gone.

By the time she had swept up the debris and finished tidying the living room, he was back. He really did live quite close.

Without any fuss, he rested the plywood on the nook in front of the window and hammered in nails until the boards were secured in place.

"Thank you," she said, fatigue beginning to override adrenaline. "I know it's late and you probably have better things to do. Like sleep."

"No need to thank me. I'm not doing it for you. Remember? It's all for Rocco."

She didn't hide the smile that surfaced. "Sorry I don't have a beer to offer you."

"I'll have what you're having, if you're in a sharing mood."

How could she say no?

She noticed he was very good at that, finding ways to turn a "no" into a "yes." Must be one of his superpowers.

Taking out a heavy glass tumbler from the cabinet, she wished she had asked him if he wanted something sooner. It was one thing to give someone a cold shoulder. Quite another to be flat-out rude. Her aunt Cecilia, Rocco's mom, would be ashamed of her lack of manners.

She poured him a nightcap and held out the glass.

As he took the tumbler from her, holding her gaze, his fingers stroked hers a tad longer than necessary. A snap of sexual awareness rocked her to the bone.

She pulled her hand from his. Took a sip of scotch as he did likewise. Tried not to stare at him. Which was impossible.

There was something magnetic about those chocolate-brown eyes staring back at her with the same intensity. Something about him overall that tugged at her.

He was tall, broad-shouldered. Had a tumble

of mahogany hair that was so thick and luxurious she ached to run her fingers through it. Down the sculpted muscle of his shoulders and arms. Not only was he good-looking, but he was also shrewd.

Still, there was more to him. But she had to figure out what it was.

"Smoother than I imagined," Brian said, his voice, like whiskey and velvet rolled into one, would have made a weaker woman shiver. He stepped closer, erasing the space between them, sucking the oxygen from her lungs. "Sweeter, too."

As he looked at her, that delicious mouth curved up in one of those smiles that tempted her to believe his good-natured friendly style was genuine.

Her brain screamed at her to get away from him, cross the room, but her feet wouldn't budge, her body betraying her by leaning in. She had never experienced the allure of another person that strongly, pulling her toward him, like gravity.

The sensation was unnerving.

He dipped his head, bringing his face closer to hers.

She thought he might lower his mouth to her lips for a kiss. Her heart thundered in her chest at the prospect. But was it because she she wanted him to kiss her, or not?

His gaze fell to her mouth, his eyes darkening. He bent closer still until the whisper of his breath brushed her skin.

A quiver shot to the pit of her stomach and knotted down to her toes.

"You better get some sleep," he said. "You've got an early day tomorrow."

Her mind stuttered. "Huh?" Disappointment flared under her skin at the lack of contact she craved. Which shouldn't have been such a surprise considering it had been a long time since she'd felt the tension and heat of a man's body. An even longer time since she'd wanted to.

The real shocker was the appetite, the interest, *this* man sparked.

"USD opens at six. Doesn't it?" he asked.

"Um, yeah." Charlie nodded. She had forgotten about everything besides Brian Bradshaw, standing in her kitchen, close enough to kiss her. "I'm usually up by five fifteen."

"It'll be a busy day for me as well. I'll make some inquires, quietly investigate."

"You believe me?" Was he going to help?

"I believe something bad happened at the Olsen ranch tonight. I believe whatever is going on has now put you in danger. There'll be an investigation, but I'm the only one who can connect the dots between the two since you've decided not to make a full statement. I also believe you're not telling me everything I need to know." His voice was gentle, even understanding, instead of accusatory, not raising her hackles. "Let's meet tomorrow night. My place."

"Why are we meeting? And why at your place?"

"I'll share whatever I find out over dinner. You've got to eat. Kill two birds with one stone." His mouth hitched in a smile, and there went another zing of scintillating energy. "I'll text you my address." He slugged back the rest of his scotch, put his glass down on the counter next to her .45 SIG Sauer, grabbed his hat and strode out the door.

Without waiting for an answer.

But he hadn't asked a question. He'd simply declared they were having dinner as though it were a foregone conclusion.

The tingle still flowing through her body was a warning sign. Brian was dangerous.

Not the first time she'd sensed it. Whenever they were within arm's reach, something inside her lit up. Made her want to know more about him. Get closer to him. Something she could not afford to do.

Not with a cop.

Chapter Four

A loud horn blared. Brian jackknifed upright. His ears rang as his gaze flew around. He was still in his truck. Parked out front of Charlie's place. Early morning sunlight poured through the rolled-down windows. Charlie stared at him, standing on the running board of his truck with her hand bearing down on his horn.

His blood surged at the sight of her. Right along with his blood pressure. "Stop it," he snapped.

Charlie removed her hand from the horn. "Morning." She handed him a disposable cup of piping hot coffee, black. "Imagine my surprise when I leave for run and find you here."

"What time is it?" He wiped the sleep from his eyes.

She glanced at her smartwatch. "Five forty-five. A better question is, what are you doing camped outside of my house? Since you're in the same clothes, I presume you were here all night."

He sipped the coffee. Scalded his tongue. A string of curses flew from him.

"Oh, my." Charlie batted her lashes. "I thought your brand of superhero was PG. No foul language permitted."

Every time he looked at her his thoughts nose-dived straight into the gutter. Definitely X-rated. He'd been in the company of beautiful women before, dated a few, too, but there was something about Charlie that kept him spellbound. "Goes to show how little you know about my brand."

He blew on the coffee and tried again. The hit of caffeine was just what he needed.

"You didn't answer my question." She raised an eyebrow. "Do I need to lay on the horn again to clear your head?"

"You wouldn't dare."

She reached for the steering wheel. "Want to test me?"

No. He did not.

The sun broke through the clouds, framing Charlie in an ethereal light. Made her look like an angel. A fallen one sent to corrupt him.

Brian had always had a thing for feisty blondes, but he wasn't sure why out of all the ones in the great state of Wyoming, or even in the world, he was so fiercely attracted to her.

But without a doubt, he was.

"It wasn't safe for you to spend the night in your house," he said. "Someone tried to kill you. Same shooter could've easily returned. I noticed your alarm system, but now you're missing a window. I wouldn't have been able to sleep worrying about you. Trying to get you to see reason seemed like it'd be a waste of time. You can be obstinate."

She folded her arms across her chest. "I prefer to be called headstrong."

Semantics. Same outcome. She wouldn't have listened to him.

A yawn scratched up his throat.

She propped her forearm on the door. "How many nights do you plan on sleeping out here?"

"Until you get your window fixed." He took another glorious sip of coffee. "Or you take pity on me by staying somewhere else." Stretching, he groaned. "This isn't the best sleeping arrangement for my back."

She pushed her pink lips out into a pout. "I'm not big on pity." She patted his unshaven cheek. "For myself anyway. I'll see what I can muster for you," she said, flashing a smile.

He couldn't help but return it. The grin spreading wider on her face, the feel of her palm on his skin, that electric thing always between them crackling with a new kind of energy.

"How kind of you," he quipped.

"Blasphemy. I don't have a kind bone in my body," she said with a wink. "I'm all fire and ice."

With either one, when it came to Charlie, he got the feeling he was going to get burned. "To be forewarned is to be forearmed. I'll be sure to handle you with care." He turned the key in the ignition, starting his engine. "See you tonight. Let's say seven thirty."

"No can do." She stepped down from the foot rail. "I don't close USD until nine. Call me with an update. No need for me to stop by for dinner."

Under normal circumstances, if this was a date, Brian would have offered to bring dinner to her at the self-defense school.

Tonight, dinner was about work. He needed her face-to-face, on his territory, where he could control the environment, get her to lower her guard. It was the easiest way to find out what she was hiding.

"You can. And you will. If you want to know what I discover." He knew how to dangle a carrot.

Charlie laughed at that. Still, she seemed to be considering it. "Who knew Captain America could play hardball?"

"I keep telling you, but you're not listening." He put his truck in drive. "You've got the brand wrong, sweetheart." He winked back.

Brian espoused virtues such as honor, integrity and courage. But he wasn't as noble as a fictitious character, who followed duty despite all costs. Not anymore. Not after the things he had done in the military. The things he'd seen.

How long would it take Charlie Sharp to figure out who he was, to see the real him?

The one thing she'd gotten right so far was that he did have a superpower. Getting people to spill their secrets.

She smirked. "I'll figure something out at USD.

I wouldn't want to miss an opportunity to compare notes."

That suggested she intended to have some new information to compare.

"Go sticking your nose in the wrong place and someone is liable to chop it off," he said. "Please tell me you learned something from last night."

"I did. Don't stand in front of the window with the curtains drawn."

Not the lesson he was thinking of, but still a worthwhile one. "Seven thirty. Don't be late." With a wave, he drove off.

Punctuality was not only a sign of respect, but also a measure of trustworthiness.

Charlie could trust him, even if she didn't believe it. He needed to know if it was a two-way street. Right now, he had serious doubts.

About her.

THIS WAS THE third window installation service Charlie had contacted. Everyone's response was the same. "Are you sure you can't replace it any sooner?" she asked, not wanting frustration to overwhelm her.

"Four weeks is the best we can do," the manager said. "A bay window with the dimensions you gave me has to be ordered. Even with putting a rush on shipping, you're looking at a month. But once we receive it, we can install it the next day."

She swallowed a groan. "Okay. I understand."

"Do you want me to order it?"

"I need the window." Even if it would take four weeks. "Go ahead."

"All right. I'll call you once it's in."

"Thank you." She hung up.

There was no way she could have Brian sleeping in his truck in front of her house one more night, much less for a month. The busted window was also a legitimate security concern that he had brought to her attention. She'd have to figure something out later.

Right now, she needed to start doing some investigating of her own. Brian might follow-through, but she couldn't rely on him. She wasn't going to take any chances of Seth Olsen getting away with this.

Charlie pushed out from behind her desk, left her office and found Dustin Lee, one of her instructors, putting away equipment from one their most popular lunchtime classes.

"Any luck on getting your window replaced sooner rather than later?" he asked.

If only. "Unfortunately, not."

"I still can't believe someone shot at you."

Neither could she. "I know. It's crazy."

The front door opened. In walked Mercy McCoy.

"Hello," the young woman said. Charlie guessed she was in her early to midtwenties. "Is Rocco here yet?" She was dressed the same as always when she came in. T-shirt and leggings, all in white.

Come to think of it, Charlie had never seen her wear anything but white. She lived on the Shining Light compound, where her father was the leader of a cult. Charlie had heard that they had a color system, where each hue held a different meaning.

She'd always wanted to ask Mercy but didn't want to make her or anyone in USD uncomfortable. This was a safe space for everyone.

"Afraid not," Charlie said. "He's not coming in today." Sometimes her cousin popped in for afternoon sessions. But she could usually rely on him to cover a couple of evening classes one night a week.

Mercy frowned, the disappointment in her eyes evident. "We were supposed to have a one-on-one training session."

It hadn't been on the schedule. Mercy had started out taking group classes, but once Rocco offered individual training, Charlie hadn't seen much of her.

"Sorry about that," Charlie said. "He's caught up with work today." She had no idea how long Rocco had been out of town. "I posted on the website that training sessions with him would be canceled until further notice."

"Internet access is limited on the compound." Mercy glanced around as if lost or as though she wasn't quite sure what to do with herself.

"If you want, Dustin can fill in and train you before the next group class."

"Oh, no." Shaking her head, Mercy eased back toward the door. "I don't want to inconvenience anyone."

"I was about to take my break, but it's no trouble," Dustin said. "Just give me ten minutes."

"That's okay. I should've checked the website for changes."

If Charlie had known about the appointment, she would've called Mercy to inform her.

"It's no problem," Dustin said. "Honest."

"I'm used to Rocco's style of teaching. I'll just wait until he gets back."

Charlie suspected that the young woman didn't want to get used to a different trainer. Whenever Rocco and Mercy were in the same room together, she stared at him like she was captivated.

Charlie would have to be blind not to see the effect her cousin had on women, but this time she thought it might be mutual. Rocco seemed equally taken by her. Mercy had a glow to her, radiating light. She was one of those natural beauties, who looked fragile on the outside, but if she was anything like her father, Marshall McCoy—Empyrean, as his acolytes called him—she was far from weak.

Underestimating Mercy would be a mistake.

"Are you sure?" Charlie asked. "You're already here."

"I'm sure."

"Sorry about the confusion," Charlie said.

"Please let him know that I stopped by." With a wave, Mercy left.

Charlie turned to Dustin. "I need a favor," she said.

"Anything. Just ask."

"Make that two favors. Can you cover things here

on your own?" It was a lot to ask. Her other trainer, Teddy Williams, had failed to show up yet again. Sometimes he came in late. Or left early. Called in sick. Regardless of the warnings she'd given him, Teddy was growing more unreliable. She understood that working at USD was only a part-time gig for him, but if this continued, she was going to have to let him go.

"Sure." Dustin didn't look enthused. "What's going on?"

"I need to take care of some things. That brings me to favor number two."

"Which is?"

"How do you feel about swapping cars?" She held up the keys to her Hellcat.

With a new gleam in his eyes, Dustin smiled. "I've been trying to get behind the wheel of that beauty since I started working here."

"Now's your chance."

"Say no more." He fished in his pocket, pulled out the keys to his SUV and handed them to her.

"I'll be back in time to close."

Once she grabbed her things, she headed to his SUV. The Jeep was ideal for surveillance. It had black-tinted windows, plenty of room to spread out and it blended in. Best of all, in case Seth noticed the vehicle, it wasn't registered to Charlie.

She tucked her hair into a baseball cap and took off. Next on her to-do list was finding Detective Olsen. Today, that might be a crapshoot.

Three weeks ago she had surveilled him, taking pictures and meticulous notes. The purpose hadn't been to ascertain if he was up to something nefarious, like now. Then it had been to see if he had a routine in order to pick the best day and time for Haley to leave him. To help a person make a smooth transition into a new life took months of preparation. Time to arrange fake credentials and build an online history. The documents that Haley would have needed weren't even ready. The plan was for Haley to disappear in twelve days once everything was in order.

While following Seth, Charlie had quickly learned two things. It was easier to do undetected if she had a tracker on his truck. The second being that the most predictable part of his schedule was in the early morning. Later in the day things got hectic, but he always hit the gym at the crack of dawn, no matter what. Beyond that, he ate at Delgado's bar and grill about three times a week. The only other places he frequented with any regularity was the local strip club out on Raven Drive—sometimes in the middle of the day or late at night since they were open from noon to 2:00 a.m.—and the station.

Charlie cruised past the police station. Brian's truck was parked out front. She took it as a hopeful sign that he was there investigating. Normally, he was at a different facility where the task force worked.

Turning the corner, she drove by the adjacent parking lot in the rear of the building and spotted

Seth's gray Chevy pickup. Charlie made a U-turn farther down the block and pulled over, where she had sight of the station as well as the lot. While she waited for him to leave, she took out her camera, which had an attached telephoto lens. She wanted proof of whatever he was up to.

Her timing couldn't have been any better. Seth shoved through the back door and strode into the lot, wearing jeans and a T-shirt. Clean-shaven. Slicked-back hair.

She wasn't sure what she had expected. Perhaps for him to appear disheveled, at the very least distressed. Certainly not groomed and undaunted with a smug smile on his face. He lit up a cigarette as he crossed the lot. She zoomed in closer on him, making sure she got a shot of the carefree grin on his face, right before he hopped into his truck.

If she was a betting a woman, she'd wager a kidney that Seth Olsen had just given the performance of his life inside the station. Playing the part of the grieving, confused husband.

What a fake and a liar. The man was no good.

It didn't take long until he drove out of the parking lot, headed in the opposite direction. Charlie put the SUV in drive and followed him, keeping as much distance as possible without losing him. Even though she was in an inconspicuous car, she didn't dare get too close. She had hoped to catch sight of another vehicle tailing him, a detective conducting a thorough investigation. But she was the only one on him.

Not surprising.

They were headed toward the outskirts of town, where it was going to be difficult to follow someone surreptitiously. With long, wide stretches of plains and winding mountain roads, there would be few, if any, cars to hide behind, but she was too stubborn to give up.

As soon as she had an opportunity, she'd put a GPS tracker back on his truck. That would enable her to keep a good mile between them without the threat of being discovered. In the meantime, she pulled into the lot of a feed store. It was the last retail shop, or much of anything, before leaving town. If Seth came back to Laramie, he'd have to take this road.

To bide some time, she used the facilities inside the store, bought some water and hunkered down in the SUV. The store had open Wi-Fi. She piggybacked off it, using the laptop that she'd brought along, and kept an eye on passing traffic while she got some work done.

Two hours later, she spotted a gray Chevy pickup. It was Seth's.

She set her laptop to the side and started the engine. Once he passed, she gave him a few seconds, then drove out. Back through town they went. Until he headed east.

The moment he turned onto Raven Drive, she knew where he was going. The audacity of it had her gritting her teeth.

Across the street from the Bare Back Gentlemen's Club, she found a place to park that offered a prime view. Rather than staying visible from the front seat, she climbed into the back of the Jeep and managed to get a few pictures of him entering the club.

Now all she could do was wait. She glanced at the time on her cell phone. If only there was some way for her to get out of dinner with Brian. Tailing Seth was a higher priority. In her gut, she knew it would lead to something, eventually. But Brian had made it clear that he wasn't going to share whatever he learned over the phone.

She needed all the pieces to put together the puzzle.

So as much as she wanted to get out of it, later tonight she had to have dinner with Bradshaw.

As BRIAN LIFTED the strainer basket from the large pot on the stove, the doorbell rang.

He looked at the time on the oven. Seven thirty on the dot. He dumped the seafood boil into an aluminum pan and shook the mound of fresh shrimp, lobster tails, crab legs, sweet corn and halved red potatoes before setting it on the outside dining table that he'd lined with newspaper. Then he wiped his hands and answered the door.

"Smells good." Charlie removed a ball cap from her head and finger-combed her hair as she stepped inside.

"Hope you're not allergic to shellfish."

"Lucky for you that I'm not."

"I should've asked." The safer choice would've been steak. "But I like to gamble from time to time."

He led the way through the main living space of his house and out the back door.

Entering the patio, she glanced at the table, where beside the food he had a bucket of ice with beers and a nice chardonnay to complement the dinner.

"Wow. Look at this spread," she said. "You made enough food for at least four."

"I like to cook large meals, so I have plenty of leftovers. Saves time in the kitchen."

She picked up the bottle of twenty-year-old Glenfiddich he'd also bought. "You even shelled out the big bucks for my favorite scotch."

It had set him back two hundred dollars, but if it got her talking, then it was worth it.

"For future reference," she said, "I only drink the stuff on rare occasions. Horrendous day. Best day ever. That sort of thing."

He was stuck on the prospect of future dinners. With her. He hoped like hell he'd get to explore the possibility. "Good to know. Have a seat."

"Mind if I clean up first?" she asked.

"No, go right ahead. Second door on the left." He indicated the hallway.

While she used the bathroom, he went back to the kitchen for the melted butter, seafood sauce and warm crusty bread. By the time he had it on the table, she reemerged. As she sat across from him, she grabbed a beer.

"I didn't think that would be your beverage of choice," he said.

"I'll have a cold brewski from time to time. But tonight, I just want to taste what you enjoy."

He smiled, unable to help it. "What's with laying on the charm?"

"I've been accused of being many things. Obstinate. Impulsive. Too smart for my own good. But charming? Never."

Tonight, they were both playing games. Did she think she had to butter him up for him to share information? Or was there more to it?

She popped the cap off her beer and took a long swig.

"Verdict?" He took a bottle of beer also and opened it.

"I like it. The pale ale will go well with the seafood. Do you eat out here often?"

"Weather permitting, every chance I get. My father made this table himself. And a few years back, I built the pizza oven."

She glanced at the outdoor kitchen that also included a grill and smoker. "Nice setup."

"Yeah." He wanted it to be nice for his parents. "I've had plenty of family meals here." Brian loved the fresh air, the land, the green landscape, surrounded by mountains. If only he had been able to do more to keep his parents living in the house longer. "Dig in."

They both helped themselves to the food, loading their plates, and began eating. He had set the table with all the utensils and tools they'd need, including wooden mallets.

She cracked crab legs, plucking out succulent meat and licking her fingers as she devoured the meal. "Did you learn anything?"

He had, but he wasn't going to rush this. "First, there's something I've been meaning to ask you."

"Oh, yeah." She tore off a piece of bread. "What's that?"

"When I offered to teach classes for free at USD, why did you turn me down without giving me a chance?"

She grunted and chewed bread. "Honestly?"

"Please." He was dying to know.

"Because you're a cop."

That stung. "So, what. Rocco is ATF. You let him help out at your school."

Munching on shrimp, she shook her head. "Not the same thing."

"Both law enforcement."

She shrugged. "Still different."

"What have you got against cops?"

She clearly had some grudge. A big one, too, if she had declined his offer to work for free based solely on that.

"I see right through this little plan of yours," she said.

"What plan is that?"

"Serving sumptuous seafood to get me talking."

She was right, but he wasn't letting on easily. "How so?"

"There's a surprising intimacy to it. The informality that comes when you eat with your hands."

It was hard to be aloof with someone while sucking tasty bits of crab from your fingers. That was the reason he'd chosen the meal instead of steaks.

Brian gave a knowing smile. "Guilty as charged." She was changing the subject. Trying to lead him down a different path. "Spill it." He kept his features soft, his tone inquisitive not defensive. "Why do you hate cops?"

"If I open that can of worms, things will get heavy, fast, and not in the way that you want."

She had no idea what he wanted. If she did, it would probably scare her off.

"I want to know you," he said. "Want you to know me." All true. "This is an important subject, considering I'm the thing you hate."

"All right. Remember you asked for this." Dropping crab legs into her bowl, she looked up at him. "My dad was a cop. He used to beat my mother. She never dared call 911 because he told her that he would make her disappear if she ever did. But the neighbors called the police a couple of times. When they showed up, they would take my dad outside, talk to him on the front lawn. Neighbors watched from their yards or from their windows. Then they'd let him go. They claimed it was because my mom wouldn't make a statement or press charges. Bottom line, calling them was pointless. I learned the hard way that blue wall of silence is real."

The same thing that had supposedly happened with Haley. At least according to Charlie.

But in this day and age, once a victim or someone

else called the police to report domestic violence, the matter was usually out of the victim's hands. If a law enforcement officer believed a crime was committed, they were obligated to arrest the alleged offender, regardless of whether the victim wanted to press charges.

Who was to say how strictly that had been enforced when Charlie was a kid?

Today, with the legislation that had been passed to protect victims of domestic violence, the law was upheld.

Of course, he wasn't so naive as to think that there weren't any cases that slipped through the cracks.

This was a small town. Seth did have a lot of friends on the force. Some who might have been inclined to look the other way. Not that Brian ever would have.

"I remember, vividly, the last time my father beat her. It was summertime. I was seven. There was a heat wave. A scorcher of a day. The cicadas were so loud, it was kind of frightening. Meat loaf for dinner set him off. Because he'd wanted fried chicken. He beat her so badly, I thought he might kill her. So, I called the cops. When they came, I finally mustered the courage to speak up. Even though my father looked at me like he wanted to strangle me, hollered at me to shut up. I kept talking, told them everything that happened. The two officers had an argument outside. One finally came back. Arrested my father. Five hours later. Five," she said, holding up her hand, "he stormed back into the house. My father snatched me out of bed by my hair. Grabbed his gun. Dragged me to their bedroom. Mom begged him not to hurt me. He looked at me with these glassy eyes, had the strangest expression. Told me that this was my fault. Then he shot my mother. Next himself. And left me alive."

To live with the memory of that horror. Surely with survivor's guilt as well. Losing both her parents in such an awful, ugly way, to be traumatized at such a young age. What a terrible thing.

"I'm so sorry you had to go through that," he said.

"That's the summer I went to live with my aunt and uncle, Rocco's parents."

It explained a lot about Charlie. Even why Rocco was the closest person to her without the two of them actually being close.

"Something like that changes you forever. Leaves an indelible mark. I've never experienced anything of that magnitude. After I lost two teammates during a dangerous mission, I almost turned into a cynical, bitter wretch." If he'd gone through what Charlie had endured, at seven, who knows what it would've done to him. As a grown man, there had been times where the darkness tugging at him had threatened to drag him under. But every day he woke up grateful, to be alive, for a chance to make a difference in the world. "Somehow, I force myself to still see the glass as half full. But it's not always easy."

He knew the situation for Charlie was far more complex.

"Enough of this pity party," she said lightly, as though they'd been making small talk. "This isn't why I'm here. Are you going to tell me what you learned? Unless you came up with nothing."

He was fascinated by more than her beauty. It was the whole package. Her mind. Her heart. Her secrets.

Her scars.

"Earlier this morning, I spoke with the fire marshal." Sawyer Powell had been helpful. "It was arson out at the Olsen house, which you already suspected. An accelerant was used. Smokeless gunpowder."

"The type of accelerant a cop would use."

She wasn't wrong there. Someone knowledgeable about firearms would've chosen it. "That's not evidence Seth was responsible for the fire. No evidence was found in Haley's car. The canines went through the debris of the house. They didn't find a body, but they did pick up some DNA. Traces of blood."

Charlie stiffened, and he could feel the tension radiating off her. "Only traces? But I saw a lot. There was so much blood."

Staring in her eyes, he believed her. "The fire destroyed quite a bit of evidence."

"What about Detective Olsen? Has he been charged?"

Brian shook his head. "No. Haley is considered a missing person. Seth has an alibi for the time in question and has been put on administrative leave."

Her brow furrowed. "What alibi?"

"Another detective who works with him." Whether they were on duty at the time was unclear, but Brian would find out for certain.

"Are you kidding me?" The tone of her voice pulled at him. "One detective protecting another. Next, you're going to say that neither of them would lie and that Seth isn't capable of murder."

People were capable of horrible things with proper motivation, under the right circumstances. Seth had worked Vice first and now Narcotics, but any smart cop would know how to get rid of a body, as well as evidence, and craft an alibi. Also, it didn't give Brian a warm and fuzzy that Seth was pals with another detective who turned out to be his alibi. But he didn't want to feed into Charlie's mistrust. "There's an experienced detective investigating. A good guy."

Although he knew the cop assigned—and there were more pros than cons with Kramer on the case—the detective had some shortcomings that made Brian wonder if it might impact the investigation. While Brian had been at the station, he hadn't been able to get the guy alone, but he needed to soon.

"Are you telling me that if Olsen is responsible, if he did something to Haley and blew up his own house to cover it up, that it's impossible for him to get away with it?"

Brian had asked himself the same question while he'd nosed around the station earlier. There were potential cracks in the system. A lot of the cops on the force had been embedded for many years and had forged deep loyalties. At times even Brian was treated as an outsider and had to struggle to break in.

"Not impossible, but improbable." He hoped.

"Are you going to wash your hands of this?" She fixed those green eyes on him. "Or are you going to look into it deeper? Will you help me?" she pleaded.

"I can't investigate a possible homicide without someone in the department catching wind of it."

"Thanks for dinner." Tossing her napkin on the table, she stood.

He got to his feet and cupped her shoulder, stopping her. "You told me that we'd compare. What did you learn?"

Charlie frowned. "When Olsen left the police station, he paid a visit to the strip club on Raven. Stayed two hours."

That wasn't a crime. "Maybe he needed to blow off steam. Disconnect for a while." Different strokes for different folks.

At the station, Seth had seemed bereft and bewildered. All the guys offered to donate clothes since he'd lost everything in the explosion, except for the things he kept in his locker at work.

"Then he went to a house on Mulberry." She gave him the exact address. "He had a key and let himself in. Can you find out who owns the place?"

"Yeah, I can, but do you have any idea how dangerous it was to follow him?"

"Somebody has to. Apparently, nobody in the

LPD cares enough to bother. I feel responsible for Haley. I was the one who convinced her to leave him and was helping her prepare. She was scared enough to be willing to upend her life and move halfway across the country. If he got wind of it and did this, then it's on me. I feel like I failed her." Charlie's gaze clung to his as everything about her softened.

The heavy weight of this, her concern for Haley along with her guilt, this striking moment of vulnerability in the impervious Charlie Sharp, shone clear in her eyes. Still, he couldn't shake the sense that there was more to this story, to her involvement, that she wasn't telling him. If only she could trust him enough to be completely honest.

A big ask that would take time. Good thing he was a patient man.

"Can you understand?" she asked in a low voice that trembled.

He sighed, knowing he was going to regret what he was about to say next. "I do and I care. I'll investigate further if you agree to back off." Her getting involved any deeper wasn't going to help resolve the case or keep Charlie safe.

"Sure," she said after a moment of hesitation. "I'll take a step back while you handle it."

Brian wanted to believe that she'd let it go. He really did, but he sensed her stubbornness was only surpassed by her determination. "Let me put the food away, grab my keys and I'll follow you home."

Another frown. "To camp out again?"

He nodded even as his back protested.

"No need," she said. "Give me the keys to Rocco's. I'll crash there until he gets back."

Brian was confident that her cousin wouldn't mind, but he'd texted his buddy earlier to be sure and got a thumbs-up. "Can I trust you to follow through? To sit on the sidelines of this and stay at Rocco's?"

Charlie gave a sad, slow smile that brought every one of his senses to red alert. "I guess you'll just have to wait and see."

Chapter Five

Guilt churned through Charlie as she maneuvered Dustin's SUV through the parking lot of Seth's gym.

It hadn't been her intention to lie to Brian when she'd agreed to keep her nose out of this. The deal had been made in good faith, albeit reluctantly. Later at Rocco's last night, she'd tossed and turned on the sofa, unable to stop thinking about Haley. Worrying about what had happened to her. Wondering whether Seth would slither free from any blame. Wishing she had the power to do something about it.

Then she realized that she did have power.

To do something no one on the police force was willing to undertake.

In the early morning lights, she spotted the gray pickup at the back of the lot.

Looked as though the creature of habit's routine hadn't changed since Charlie ran surveillance on him earlier in the year. If he did as she expected, he would spend another ten minutes pumping weights. Then wrap up with a three-mile run on the treadmill before hitting the showers. Since he was on administrative leave, she had no idea where he'd go after that.

She parked with an empty space between their vehicles, tucked a baseball cap on her head, slipped the hood from her black zip-up jacket over it and got out. Glancing around to make sure the coast was clear, she edged closer to the Chevy.

Once she was sure no one would see her, she shot around to the passenger's side and dropped to the ground near the back wheel. Planting a tracker inside a vehicle was ideal, but it took longer and circumventing an alarm system wasn't simple with a modern car. Placing it outside did run the risk of the device breaking or getting lost, but she'd had good luck in the past. She took the GPS tracker from her pocket and reached up past the wheel and mounted the magnetic box, the size of a deck of playing cards, on a flat surface on the frame. Unless he had to change the tire, he'd never see it.

Unfortunately, it wasn't a motion-activated unit that would only turn on whenever the vehicle started moving, which preserved the life of the battery. But she hoped there wouldn't be a need to follow him for months.

She got up and hopped into the SUV.

None too soon either. Seth pushed through the doors of the gym in deep conversation with another man who wore glasses. The guy had a slight build and was jumpy. Kept looking around with a nervous expression.

Charlie grabbed her camera and got a few quick shots of the two speaking.

Olsen started walking through the parking lot. He put his hand on the man's shoulder. Glasses stiffened, then nodded as he listened.

A couple more photos. Time to get out of there before he noticed her.

Now she'd be able to follow his every move. Document whatever he was up to.

The way Haley talked about her husband, Charlie had discovered one important thing about him. His hubris was his weakness. Seth Olsen thought he could do anything and get away with it. Maybe even murder.

Well, not anymore.

It HAD BEEN over a year since Brian had been in the police station two days in a row. Every time he stepped inside the building claustrophobia set in. He'd grown accustomed to being on loan to the task force, far removed from the others on the force. Having a sense of purpose that better suited his skill set. Getting to work with the FBI and ATF had broadened his horizons and had gotten him thinking about what was next in his career beyond the LPD.

Detective Kent Kramer wasn't at his desk, but Brian found him in the breakroom filling up his travel mug with coffee.

"Hey, Kent." Brian strode up to him.

"Well, look at who it is. Decided to grace us with your presence again."

The detective met his gaze. Heavy bags under his bloodshot eyes bolstered Brian's concerns. After the death of his wife in a car accident, Kent hadn't been the same. It was no secret he drowned his sorrows every night at a bar. Before Brian's assignment to the joint task force, he'd never caught the smell of alcohol on Kent's breath, but there had been times when he'd wondered if the detective had become a functioning alcoholic. Kent still could get the job done, but his drinking was also a potential liability that Brian couldn't ignore.

"I was hoping to run in to you. Alone."

"Oh, yeah," Kent said, with an easy smile. "Something little ole me can do to help you on your *special* task force?"

Kent had taken a shine to him from the beginning and had been the one to encourage Brian to go for detective early. Not quite a mentor, Kent had been more of cheerleader. Rooting him on. The first to tell him "atta boy." The only one to congratulate him on being picked as the police liaison for the task force.

"No," Brian said. "Actually, I was wondering if I might be of any assistance to you?"

Kent's brow furrowed as the smile faded. "How so?"

"I was driving by Seth's place last night," Brian said, "and saw the smoke from the fire."

"Really?" Kent smoothed a hand down over his wrinkled suit jacket. "According to dispatch, you got a report about the fire. No mention of you seeing it firsthand."

"Both, really." Brian poured himself a cup of coffee. "I was wondering why you're the only one investigating." For a case this big, involving one of their own, there should be two detectives working on it.

Kent glanced around, causing Brian to do likewise. They were alone in the room. No one was in the hallway. "I asked the lieutenant the same thing," he said, lowering his voice. "Apparently, it's complicated. This doesn't look good for Seth, you know, considering his first wife, Linda, died under suspicious circumstances."

Brian wasn't aware that he'd been married before. "What happened to her?"

"Too much wine. Slipped down the stairs. Broke her neck. Coroner ruled it an accident."

"But Seth lived in a one-story ranch."

Kent shook his head. "They used to live in Linda's house. Massive place. Three levels."

"Do you remember her blood alcohol content?"

"Looked it up once I got this case. She had a .30 BAC."

Brian whistled. That was high enough to severely impair walking, even speech. At .08 a person was considered intoxicated.

"After she died, he sold the house," Kent said. "Used the proceeds to stop his family ranch from going into foreclosure. Seth said that it was the only good thing that came out of her death. That she was his angel taking care of him from the beyond."

"That doesn't explain why you're the only detective on this." If anything, that gave even more reasons as to why this was a two-person investigation.

Kent's gaze swept the hallway. He waited until an officer passed by. "Rumor has it there are dirty cops in the LPD."

Brian had heard rumblings of the same and presumed the new police chief, Wilhelmina Nelson, had been brought in to clean up the problem before it was verified as credible and made headlines. One more reason Brian had been grateful to be assigned elsewhere. But the chief was in for an uphill battle.

If there were dirty cops, Vice and Narcotics would be a good place to start looking for them. The odds were there would be others at different levels, working in various areas. A tight-knit group.

Kent took a gulp of his coffee. "Chief Nelson told the lieutenant that she doesn't want anyone close to Seth working on the case. You're looking at the one detective who isn't, besides yourself. He's bosom buddies with all the others."

Laramie was a small town. The size of the entire police force was tiny compared to a single precinct in a large city like New York or Chicago.

"Internal Affairs is going to get involved," Kent said. "They're sending someone down from Cheyenne next week. Until then, it's just me."

"Have you made any headway? Got any leads?"

Kent added cream and sugar to his coffee. "One dead end after another so far. No pun intended. Seth claims if anything happened to his current wife that her boyfriend is behind it. I talked to the guy. He clammed up as soon as I mentioned the name Olsen. Refused to say anything else. But he denied being Haley's lover, and he's got a solid alibi that checks out." Kent took another furtive glance toward the corridor. "Which is more than I can say for Seth."

More surprising news. "I thought Colvin was his alibi."

Sipping his coffee, Kent nodded. "Yeah. Supposedly. But they weren't on duty at the time. I can't verify that they were even together or what they were doing. I've only got Colvin's and Seth's word to go on."

Wonderful. "What's the alleged boyfriend's name?" Brian asked.

Tipping his head to the side, Kent gave him a wry look. "Why?"

"Maybe I can take another pass at him for you. It can't hurt."

"Listen, you're the only other detective I'd even consider talking to about this. It's a big mess. Nothing adds up. My gut tells me this one is not going to end well. As much as I could use someone else on this case with me, it's got to be official. If you want more information or intend to question suspects, you have to get the lieutenant's blessing. Then I'll be happy to share everything I've got, and you'll be free to take a crack at the alleged boyfriend. But you should know that Olsen has some serious connections in town. You won't be doing yourself any favors hitching a ride on this circus."

Brian gave him a two-finger salute. If Kent was

already seeing red flags, the need for a second detective investigating was essential. And urgent. IA's involvement was a good sign, but a lot could happen between now and their arrival. Evidence had already been destroyed in the fire. Who was to say what else could happen.

Carrying his cup of coffee, Brian made his way to the lieutenant's office. He rapped his knuckles on the door.

Lieutenant Malcolm Jameson looked up from the computer. "Bradshaw." He beckoned for him to enter. "Surprised to see you. What can I do for you?"

Brian closed the door behind him. "Can I speak frankly?"

"I wouldn't have it any other way." The lieutenant gestured for him to take a chair. "Are you having a problem on the task force? Supervisory Agent Nash Garner speaks very highly of the work you're doing over there."

"That's nice to know and no, I'm not having any problems. I heard about the investigation regarding Detective Olsen and the disappearance of his wife. I understand the situation is complicated, but Kramer would welcome a partner on this."

Lieutenant Jameson pressed his lips into a thin, hard line. "He's the only one Chief Nelson would sign off on. We need to make sure there isn't a conflict of interest in the investigation. Kramer is seasoned and capable. Besides, he only has to manage a few more days. IA will be here soon enough."

"Do you think the chief would sign off on me?"

"Don't you already have an assignment? A fairly high-profile one at that."

Since Brian had joined the force, he kept his nose to the grindstone, never taking vacation days or calling in sick. Only handling family affairs in his spare time. Nash had been pushing him to take some time off. So when Brian had finally asked this morning, his last-minute request had been approved.

"As luck would have it, I can be spared for a few days. I've got the free time. Rather than slack off, why not put me on the case?"

The lieutenant leaned back in his chair and folded his hands on the desk. "I have to admit I'm surprised you've taken such a keen interest in this."

"If my wife went missing and my house blew up, I'd want it to be all hands on deck. This is a two-person case, yet only one detective is working on it."

Jameson narrowed his eyes. "I still haven't figured you out yet. What drives you to push so hard. Ambition? Accolades? Some other angle? I know you don't do it for the paycheck."

Smiling, Brian lowered his head. He could offer the truth. That the driving force in him was simple— a call to serve. To protect. To see justice served. Never to miss the opportunity to fulfill his purpose.

Instead, he said, "I owe Kent. If not for him, I wouldn't be a detective. He's still going through a rough patch and needs a partner until IA gets here. I'd like to do it."

The lieutenant nodded. "I can respect that. It's good that you've had distance with the department for a while. You've got a reputation for getting along with everyone, and yet, not really being pals with anyone." Then he frowned. "Don't you play football with Seth and a few of the others? Yeah," he said, as if remembering now. "You scored the winning touchdown in the annual game against the fire department."

"The season is about to start back up. This week in fact. I can make excuses not to participate. I only played for fun and the extra exercise. Sometimes we grabbed a drink afterward. I assure you there's no conflict of interest."

After a moment of consideration, he said, "Okay." He picked up the phone. "If Chief Nelson says yes, which I think she will, you're Kent's partner. Temporary basis. Avoid coming to the station. No one will know you're on this. It's best to keep it that way. And when football starts up again, you should play like you normally would. You never know what you might learn."

"Sure, I can do that."

CLICK. CLICK.

Charlie snapped photos of Seth leaving Delgado's. He'd finished having dinner with a man she recognized. The guy had a couple of well-placed ads touting him as the sharpest real estate agent in the Cowboy State.

Pretty big claim if you asked her.

After Seth climbed into his truck, she threw the SUV into drive and followed her target. Luck had been on her side this morning when she'd found Seth at the gym. From there, tailing him all day had been simple, even if it had turned up absolutely nothing so far. Nonetheless, she'd keep at it, tracking him, photographing whatever she could.

When the time was right, she'd come clean to Brian and admit to him that sitting on the sidelines wasn't her style. There had to be different terms they could agree on where he'd still help look into this.

Sighing, Charlie turned down Raven.

Good grief, again?

Part of her considered not even bothering to follow him to the strip club, but she'd devised the plan to see what eventually turned up. That required her to stick to it, no matter how dull or repetitive the task.

After she parked in the same spot she'd found yesterday, she took a few pictures of him entering the club. Then she settled into the back seat of the SUV with no idea how long the wait could be.

This was dull work, but her fingers were crossed that it would pay off in the end.

An hour later and one power bar eaten, the front door of the club swung open. A redhead with voluminous, curly hair strutted out, wearing a robe that was tied closed and sky-high heels. Charlie slumped down in the back seat, ready to dismiss her until she realized the woman was making a beeline straight over to the SUV.

What in the world?

Setting the camera to the side, Charlie considered hopping in the front behind the wheel and taking off, but she'd already been made. Better to find out what the woman wanted.

The redhead marched up to the vehicle and knocked on the driver's side rear window. "Get out of the car."

"Excuse me?"

"You heard me. Get out. Right now."

Questions tumbled through Charlie's mind. The woman posed no physical threat, yet Charlie had a bad feeling about this. It wasn't often that she followed people and staked out a place, but this was the first time something like this had ever happened.

Bang, bang, bang.

The jarring sound came from the roof of the vehicle, snatching Charlie's attention to the passenger's side.

A tall, beefy man stood at the other window. Wearing a black T-shirt that exposed sculpted biceps and black pants, he was clearly a bouncer. He must have left the club out a different door and crept around.

They'd gotten the drop on her.

"You heard the woman," he said in a deep baritone voice. "Out of the car."

Her options seemed limited but doing as they ordered wasn't at the top of her list of preferences. "I'll leave, okay," Charlie said, climbing into the front seat.

As she fumbled for the keys, the redhead drew something from one of the robe's pockets that glinted in the fading light of day. It was a switchblade. "I bet I can flatten two tires before you pull off," the woman said, holding up the knife. "What's it going to be? You get out and we chat, or you get flat tires?"

That narrowed her choices down to two. Both undesirable. What did they want from her?

Had Seth spotted her and sent them to check her out?

Charlie glanced over at her purse where her gun was stashed. Drawing it might dial up the tension unnecessarily. If need be, she could disarm the woman and take on the bouncer. Violence was always a last resort for her. She unlocked the door and did as they demanded. "Is there a problem?" she asked, raising her palms in a conciliatory gesture.

"That's what I'm here to find out." The redhead pointed the tip of the blade at Charlie and propped her other hand on her hip. "This is the second day I've seen you scoping the place out. The last time someone cased the club, me and two other girls were robbed after our shifts."

The aggressive approach now made sense and was even warranted.

"This is a misunderstanding." One that could hopefully be cleared up easily and quickly. "I'm not casing the club or planning to rob anyone."

"Then why are you out here?"

"I'm following a husband." Charlie gestured over her shoulder to the back seat of the car, where the camera was visible.

The redhead looked inside. "All right. I believe you. Now, that'll be fifty bucks for each of us."

Charlie lowered her hands. "What exactly am I paying for?"

"Our silence." The redhead smiled. "Otherwise, Hammer," she said, pointing to the bouncer, "is going to tell every dude inside to be on the lookout for you, along with your description, the make, model, color and license number of your car."

This was a shakedown. How many private investigators had they put through the same process?

With a groan, Charlie got her purse and fished out what little cash she had. "It's all I have. Eighty bucks will have to suffice."

"This will do." They divided the cash between them. The bouncer headed back to the club while the woman stayed. "The husband inside yours?"

"No."

"What's his name?"

Charlie folded her arms. "I'd rather not say."

"And I'd rather that you did. Believe it or not, I'm all about women helping women."

A harsh chuckle flew out of Charlie's mouth. "Forgive me for not believing you, considering you just extorted me for money."

"We all got to make a living, sweetheart. Even you're getting paid by the hour to sit out here with your camera."

"This is pro bono for me. A friend of mine is missing, and I'm trying to figure out if her husband is responsible."

Something passed over the woman's face, perhaps a flicker of curiosity or concern. "Most of the men in there treat us like meat. Disposable. Not like working women, trying to pay their bills, who deserve respect. I don't owe any of them anything. What's his name?"

There were a hundred reasons not to trust her and if any of them were valid, then forty dollars was going to buy her silence anyway. "Seth Olsen," Charlie said, figuring she had more to gain than to lose.

The redhead reeled back. "Haley is missing?"

"You know her?"

"Yeah." She nodded. "We're friends."

Friends? Charlie hadn't seen that one coming.

"We can't talk out here," the woman continued, glancing back across the street. "Drive around to the back of the club and park behind the dumpster. Wait about thirty minutes. Give me a chance to do my performance and I'll come out afterward."

"Okay." Charlie opened the car door as a thought struck her. "Hey, I didn't get your name?"

"Aubrey. Who are you?"

"I'm Charlie."

Once she had parked in the rear of the building, where Aubrey had told her, it was the longest thirty minutes of her life as she waited. Hard to believe that Haley was friends with Aubrey, stripper and extortionist. Haley was always Miss Prim-and-Proper. As a housewife, she had plenty of time to volunteer at the hospital and for social clubs like the Kiwanis, the cache of crocheters, and running the weekly bingo game down at the VFW—Veterans of Foreign Wars.

This didn't fit her image. Then again, when Aubrey was fully clothed and not wielding a knife, maybe she enjoyed crocheting, too.

Charlie's pulse spiked when the redhead pushed through the back door, once again wearing a robe.

The staccato *click-clack* of Aubrey's heels echoed in the alleyway as she approached the vehicle. She hopped in the passenger's seat and shut the door.

One question kept repeating in Charlie's head. "How did you and Haley meet?" she asked, hoping it didn't come across as offensive.

"At the club," Aubrey said. "Haley used to work here. That's how she met Seth. She caught his eye and made sure to keep his attention. At first, he was adoring, even sweet. She reeled him in, and he swept her off her feet. After they got married, he made her quit. Haley didn't mind. She thought he just didn't want her taking her clothes off for other men, but soon enough she learned that he wouldn't let her get a job anywhere. Insisted that she stay at home."

He wanted her isolated, alone and completely dependent on him for money. "That's the classic behavior of an abuser."

"You know?" Aubrey turned toward her and leaned against the door. "That he beats her?"

Charlie nodded.

"Once they got engaged, he became controlling." Aubrey wrung her hands. "I told her he wasn't going to stop after they exchanged vows. Something like that always gets worse. But she wouldn't listen. She thought he was her Prince Charming."

No such thing. A perfect example of why Charlie

hated fairy tales. Rather than be a damsel in distress, she believed in rescuing herself.

"What happened to Haley?" Aubrey asked.

"I don't know. I'm trying to piece it together."

"He used to tell her that if she didn't do as she was told that he'd make her disappear. I guess he finally made good on that promise. Not the first time, either. You know his first wife died? The newspaper said it was a tragic accident. Stated Seth had been cleared of any suspicion."

The coincidence of two women Seth had been married to snatched out of his life—one an accident, the other disappeared—was too strong, too far a stretch to be happenstance. Or to be ignored.

"Did you ever hear him threaten Haley?" Charlie asked. "Witness the abuse firsthand?"

Aubrey shook her head. "No. Only what Haley told me."

Then the cops would dismiss it, calling it hearsay. "When was the last time you spoke to her?"

"It's been months. Not since Seth started coming to the club almost daily. I noticed he started paying less attention to the girls while he's here. He's always meeting with somebody. This is like his second office. I told Haley about it. She asked me to spy on him. But it was too dangerous. I told her no. Then she stopped talking to me. I ran into Rafe a few weeks ago. Asked him how she was doing. But he hadn't seen her in ages, either."

"Who's Rafe?"

"Rafael Martinez. Her *friend*," Aubrey said, using air quotes on the last word.

Maybe Brian was right about a third party. "Was Rafe her lover?"

Aubrey shrugged. "I don't know for sure, but I kind of got that feeling. Like she was relying on him to help her break free of Seth. Haley had this way with men, of luring them in, making them feel special. As though they were the center of the universe. When she wanted to be, she was mesmerizing."

"Any idea where I can find Rafe?"

"He works at the floral shop on Grand Avenue."

"Thanks for talking to me." Charlie was sure that this conversation could put Aubrey at risk.

"If you really want to thank me, don't come back here again. Not unless it's to tell me that you found Haley. Or Seth has been arrested."

Chapter Six

Charlie pulled into a spot a couple of doors down from The Prickly Poppy floral shop. She took off her baseball cap and ran her fingers through her hair before she climbed out and headed for the door.

"Please tell me this is a happy coincidence," a familiar male voice said from behind her just as she reached the shop, "and not something that's going to stick in my craw."

Swallowing a sigh, she turned on her heel and faced Brian. "Let's call it a coincidence and leave it at that." Although surprisingly, she was happy to see him.

"Are you here to buy flowers?" he asked, drawing close enough that she had to tip her head back to meet his eyes.

A quiver ran through her belly, but she steeled herself against it.

Her first instinct was to lie. It would've been simpler, avoiding the discussion that they needed to have, but Brian had been a stand-up guy with her to this point. As far as she knew, he hadn't betrayed her trust. Not only did she owe him honesty, but he also had an easy way about him that made opening up more comforting than cringeworthy. Which was a first for her.

"No, I'm not here for flowers," she admitted.

"Is the reason going to—"

"Stick in your craw?" she said, finishing his question. "Yeah, I think it will."

Brian stiffened. "We had an agreement. I've kept my end of the bargain. I'm now assigned to the case. Free to investigate. While you're lying to me, running around, still endangering yourself."

"I thought I could do it. Sit back, do nothing besides wait. Turns out, I'm not built that way. I'm sorry. I didn't mean to lie to you last night."

He gazed down at her. "I'm only trying to keep you safe."

Even though it was obvious he was perturbed, it was the worry in his eyes that made her look down at her feet and swallow around the sudden lump in her throat. It didn't help that he was genuinely nice. And downright sexy.

She'd never been much for cowboys, usually going for the bad boys instead. But a Stetson and jeans looked really hot on him. He was so clean-cut with the kind of wholesome qualities that made her want to get him dirty.

The dangerous combination was beginning to wear her down.

"Whose car are you driving?" he asked, glancing at the SUV.

"It belongs to Dustin, one of my trainers."

"What happened to your Hellcat?"

"Nothing." Shoving her hands in the pockets of her jeans, she straightened. "Now, please stop asking questions that you won't want to hear the answer to." At least Rocco knew better. "I'm not used to this." She waved a hand between them. "Sharing. Cooperating. Making deals and sticking to them."

"It's called working on a team."

He'd hit the nail on the head.

"Yeah," she said. "Not really my forte. I usually go it alone."

"I get it, but you're going to have to figure out how to meet me halfway. I'm putting my neck on the line here, and I don't feel like it's a two-way street."

Tension knotted in her shoulders. "What do you mean?"

"You're not willing to go out on a limb with me. Instead, you're still keeping things from me. I need to know what you're hiding that might help me put it all together."

Her gut clenched. She didn't like that he could see through her, but he had no idea what he was asking of her.

"Charlie." Brian took her by the arm, his grip soft, almost soothing, like his voice. "I don't expect you to spill all your secrets to me on the sidewalk. But telling me the truth is the first part of what I need from you."

The first? "What's the second?"

"You're going to keep digging into this, aren't you?"

She nodded. "I have to do everything that I can."

"I realize that now. So, I'm going to need you stay at my place while you do," he said, and Charlie pulled her arm free. "Before you give me a hard time over the idea, you need to understand that if you insist on putting yourself in danger, then this is the only way I can keep you safe."

"I can protect myself." She'd packed her gun along with other essentials when she'd gone to Rocco's. If ever there was a time to carry it with her, it was now.

He sighed. "Someone already shot at you. You keep poking around, they might try again. If you're with me, you won't be an easy target like you would be alone at Rocco's." His gentle tone made her chest hurt. "Those are the new terms. Nonnegotiable. Or I stop sharing information."

Charlie's mouth dropped open.

How could he box her in like this with an ultimatum? She stepped back, away from him, anger building against her rib cage despite his calm, caring approach. All she could do was glare.

"I'll give you time to think about it while I question Rafe Martinez."

"I'm coming with you," she said.

"I can't have you tagging along with me. This is official. You're staying out here. And while you sit back, try to gain some perspective. Working with me is your best option, but I require full disclosure."

"As well as me sleeping in your bed."

He quirked an eyebrow. "Was that a Freudian slip? I never said anything about *my* bed. I was thinking you'd sleep in the guest room, but whatever you prefer. You're welcome between my sheets anytime." An irritating grin tugged at his mouth as he leaned toward her. Closer and closer. So close that she smelled his aftershave—sandalwood and cedar. "You don't need to fear it or fight it." His breath was warm against her ear.

"What's that?" she asked, his proximity fuzzing up her thoughts.

He met her eyes and brushed her cheek with the back of his hand. "Chemistry."

That one word rang true as a bell, echoing inside of her, dredging up all the loneliness she often tamped down out of habit. A visceral attraction and curiosity and that stupid tingle suppressing her rational mind drew her to him.

She was loath to admit it, but this thing between them was combustible.

Their *chemistry*, and everything about Brian Bradshaw, scared her senseless.

"Other options besides fight or flight," he said softly, his lips an inch from hers, his breath a caress on her face. "More pleasurable ones, too." He cupped a hand around her neck and pulled her mouth to his.

All the reasons not to get close to Brian, that this was a mistake, melted away. The kiss was a slow, hot, all-encompassing thing that was more persuasive than possessive. Everything about it, his warm mouth, his tongue sliding against hers, his rough hand holding her still, was right. As if every interaction prior had been leading up to this moment—stacked dominoes waiting to fall.

But when he broke the kiss, gently easing his body from hers, doubt flowed in like the tide. Waves of it telling her this was wrong.

She only stood there, the breath backing up in her lungs, her pulse throbbing hard and thick. No one had ever kissed her like that, with so much... What was the word for a perfect mix of fire and sweetness? It was like the world had turned upside down, the aftershock leaving her a quivering mess. Her insides turned to jelly.

Brian didn't move. Didn't say anything. Not that he needed to because his hot, penetrating stare spoke volumes.

She glanced away. Cleared her throat. "I'll wait here." Turning, she licked her lips, tasting him again, and went back to the SUV. She leaned against the vehicle and folded her arms across her chest so he wouldn't see that her hands were trembling.

As Brian opened the door to the shop, there was a little chime, and he stepped inside.

The memory of the kiss tingled across her lips. One little kiss and she was struggling to steady herself. What would happen if she slept with him?

He had left her with her brain a little scrambled and two big demands to consider. Both had been issued out of his sense of decency, his nobility—which she was finding harder to question and even harder to resist. Her mind worked overtime to clear it of thoughts of him.

One thing stood out in the haze. The way Aubrey spoke about Haley, as a mesmerizing stripper capable of making a man feel like the center of the universe.

The meek, mousy woman who had skulked into the Underground Self-Defense school all of two months ago, desperate to claim some power over her life sounded like a different woman. Was it possible that Seth had beaten the light out of her, turning her into a husk of the person she used to be?

Or had Haley been acting, playing a sick game?

The florist shop door opened with a chime and Brian strode out. From his grim expression, the conversation hadn't gone well.

"That was fast," she said.

"Because he wouldn't talk to me. He already spoke to another detective and didn't have anything to add to his statement."

"Now what?" she asked. "Any ideas for a next step?"

He rested a shoulder against the car, facing her and hooked his thumbs in his belt. "Did you make a decision?"

She had decided. "For future reference, I hate ultimatums," she said, and his mouth curved a little bit. "But we'll do it your way." Getting shot at wasn't a pleasant experience. If staying with Brian reduced the likelihood of it happening again, then she'd go along with his plan. As for telling him about her illicit activities, maybe that was for the best. Better to scare him off now. Nip this thing between them in the bud once and for all.

She only prayed she didn't end up in jail as a result.

"Then the next step is for you to give it a try with Rafe," he said.

"I thought he wouldn't talk."

"Not to a cop." Brian brushed strands of hair from her face, those chocolate-brown eyes of his direct. "I think you two can build a rapport on common ground," he said in that husky scrape of a voice that sent a tingle down her spine.

Her gaze dropped to his mouth. Just for a second until she remembered Rafe. "I'll give it a go."

"We'll meet back up at my place," he said, heading to his truck.

"Where are you off to?"

"You wanted me on the case. Now that I am, I've got to investigate. I looked up the address you gave me to the house on Mulberry. It's owned by an off-shore LLC. The more I dig, the murkier it gets. It's not as easy to hide your identity as it once was, but the owner has done an impressive job. I'm going to speak to an attorney. See what I can find out."

She nodded. "Okay, and so you know, I won't make it to your house until late. I've got to lock up USD tonight." Teddy was a no-show again and Dustin had a life. Unlike her. She couldn't expect him to work her grueling hours, especially with little advance notice. With the way things were going, following Seth whenever she could, she was going to have to close USD. Perhaps for a few hours every day. Maybe even for a whole day.

"Good luck in there," Brian said, tipping his hat to her.

She entered the shop. The chime sounded. Fragrant, cool air perfumed by flowers curled around her. She met the gaze of the man who was looking at her from behind the counter.

"Hello," he said, snipping a stem of a rose. "Welcome to The Prickly Poppy. Is there something I can help you with today?"

She went up to counter. His name tag read *Rafe*. "I hope so. I'm Charlie Sharp."

"I know who you are." His smile faltered. "You own Underground Self-Defense."

"Haley attended classes there. We're friends. She went missing two days ago."

His features tightened into a wary expression. He set down the shears. "The cops told me. Was that your buddy who was just in here, the one with the badge?"

"I don't like cops. Don't trust them. It worries me that Haley's husband is one and now, she's disappeared."

He gave a slight nod. "What does that have to do with me?"

"I heard you two were friends. Anything you can tell me about Haley might help."

"We used to be friends, but I haven't talked to her in a while."

"It was my understanding that you two were close," she said. "What happened?"

"If Seth finds out that I told anyone—"

"He won't. I promise." She hoped he believed her. "Why did you stop being friends?"

"Last February, that maniac caught me outside, in the back of the shop as I was locking up one night. He was wearing a ski mask," Rafe said. "He beat me up and told me to stay away from his wife. If I went near her again, he'd kill me."

Now she understood why he was being tight-lipped with the police. "That never should've happened to you." Charlie put her hand on his. "Did he say her name? Are you sure it was him?"

"He didn't need to say her name," Rafe scoffed. "I knew who he meant. Recognized his voice. Have nightmares about it."

"I hate to pry, but were you and Haley having an affair?"

Lowering his gaze, Rafe shook his head.

"You can tell me if you were. Her husband is a monster." A wife beater and possibly a murderer. "He treated her like garbage."

"We weren't. Haley needed someone to lean on, to listen to her problems. We clicked. You know?" Rafe said. "There was this one moment when we were having drinks, she did kiss me. It caught me by surprise. I wasn't expecting it. I'm gay, and thought she knew. After I told her, we laughed it off. No big deal. I grew to love Haley. It was hard not to once you got to know her. But it was platonic. I tried to explain to her husband, but he didn't give me a chance."

"Do you know if she was involved with anyone else?" Charlie asked.

"Not while we were friends. I think she would've confided in me if she had been."

"Did Haley mention anything about leaving Seth?"

"Only that she wanted to, but she was scared. I was the one who suggested she take classes at the USD. Then Haley got it into her head to get her friend Aubrey to spy on Seth at the strip club. Something shady was going on. Haley figured that if Aubrey could find some dirt on him that it would give her leverage."

"Don't you mean Haley asked her, but Aubrey refused?"

"No." Rafe shook his head. "They would meet up once a week. Aubrey would tell her everything she found out."

"Are you certain?"

"Positive. Sometimes they spoke in the back here. Or at the pastry shop, Divine Treats. Even the library. Haley was excited about it. Not just the clandestine nature, but it seemed like she might actually get something on Seth."

But why would Aubrey lie?

It was getting harder to figure out who was lying and who was telling the truth.

"How many times did they meet?" Charlie asked.

Rafe shrugged. "I have no idea. After her husband's violent warning, I cut ties with Haley. I know she needed me, and I feel bad about doing it, abandoning her, but I felt like I had no other choice."

The look in his eye was familiar.

Charlie was doing everything in her power to push beyond the crushing sense of failure, but it was rooted deep. The only thing that would ease the mounting pressure was getting answers to her questions.

Chapter Seven

Holding a bag of pastries from Divine Treats, Brian knocked on the office door of assistant district attorney, Melanie Merritt.

She looked up from a stack of papers on her desk, her gaze bouncing from his face to the white paper bag. She groaned. "I told you to stop bribing me for favors. My waistline can't afford it."

With a chuckle, he strode in and removed his hat.

Melanie was savvy, smart, sophisticated and easy on the eyes. The kind of workaholic who only took a break to eat, sleep and exercise.

"Who are you trying to kid?" He placed the bag in the center of her desk. "You're more fit than I am. Besides, you probably didn't even have lunch." *Busy* was the woman's middle name.

A twinge of guilt coursed through him for imposing on her.

Mel frowned. "Got me there. I haven't had anything to eat since breakfast. Unless you count my steady stream of coffee."

"I do not. Can't subsist off caffeine."

"Says who?" Opening the bag, she peered inside and melted at the sight and smell. "My favorite."

A chicken, spinach and artichoke puff pastry tart. The last time she had spent countless hours helping the task force on a case, he noticed how much she enjoyed them.

"I even had them heat it up for you," he said.

"You're going to make some lucky woman very happy one day."

He was working on it. "Can you spare a few minutes?"

"You've come bearing gifts. How can I say no?" She gestured for him to sit.

"I'm working a missing person case, trying to piece things together. A possible suspect was seen at a house." He gave her the address and she made a note. "Tried to find out who owns the place. Got the name of an offshore limited liability company. NHB, LLC. I thought it would be simple to see who was behind it." The Corporate Transparency Act was designed to prevent true anonymity. The CTA maintained a registry of actual owners that was only available to law enforcement, not to the public. "When I looked them up in the database, an offshore holding company was listed."

"Well, the CTA only requires all US registered corporations, LLCs and similar entities to report beneficial ownership."

"So, it's foreign owned?"

"Maybe. Maybe not." She leaned back in her chair. "There are loopholes for both. A beneficial owner is one who owns at least a twenty-five percent equity stake. Say there were five individuals, if each owned twenty percent, they could get around the requirement. Another way is to bury their identities in layers. One offshore LLC behind another and then a holding company after that. Either way, it took someone with legal expertise, who was extremely well-versed in navigating the cracks in the system to do it."

"How do I find out who owns it?"

"Without a subpoena?" she asked.

He nodded. "For now. It's possible a dirty cop is involved. I need this to stay quiet."

"That's going to be tricky. It'll also take time. But I can look into for you."

"When? Are you going to do it instead of sleeping?" He was only half-joking.

She smiled. "I've got to pay you back for this tart some way, don't I?"

Not enough pastries in the entire Cowboy State to earn her assistance. "Thanks. I appreciate it." He stood and headed for the door.

"Brian," she said, stopping him. "You should be careful. It's not often that I've seen insulated layers like this."

He put on his hat. "But you have seen it before?"

She nodded. "The only time I've seen double or triple layering like this is when the cartel has been involved. Throw a dirty cop into the mix and this could blow up in your face. Literally. Watch your back out there."

CHARLIE LOCKED THE front door of USD for the night and checked the GPS tracker on her phone again. This evening Seth had spent time in Centennial and Woods Landing-Jelm. Both towns were a thirty-minute drive from Laramie. She recalled Seth had trekked out there three weeks ago when she'd followed him while prepping for Haley. At the time, she hadn't been concerned with what he was doing, only *where* and *when*. Now she wished she knew what he was doing out there, but she'd had to relieve Dustin earlier.

The exact addresses were logged in the GPS history. Maybe she could ask Brian to research them.

Now, it appeared that Seth was at the house on Mulberry again.

She had enough sense not to go skulking around the place in the darkness by herself. But that didn't mean she couldn't stake it out from down street for a bit. She locked the back door of USD and strode into the parking lot.

As she started up the SUV, which Dustin had agreed to let her hang on to for a couple more days, her stomach grumbled. She hadn't eaten since noon. On the way to Mulberry, she swung through a drive-through. Ordered a double cheeseburger and fries, but she denied herself the milkshake she was craving in lieu of water.

The warm, hearty smell that permeated the car was divine. She dug french fries from the bag and noshed while she made her way to the house.

The lights were on inside. Out front were two cars

behind Seth's truck that hadn't been there the last time. Shadows moved behind the drawn curtains. Three, possibly four individuals were inside from what she could see.

There weren't many cars on the street. Most were parked in driveways.

Charlie chose a spot across the street and two houses down behind a sedan. She set her camera on top of her duffel bag, ready to take pictures if an opportunity presented itself. Biting into the burger, she stayed focused on the house, silently nibbling on her food until there was nothing left.

As she wiped her mouth, the front door opened. Three men strode out, including Olsen.

Chucking the napkin in the paper bag with the rest of her trash, she grabbed her camera and zoomed in on the men. She took pictures of them talking while they walked down the front steps. At the sidewalk, they spoke for a few minutes. The one with close-cropped dark blond hair pointed back to the house. Another glanced at his watch, the one who was balding and had a bit of a belly.

Seth nodded at them and waved goodbye. He started toward his truck.

She got pictures of the license plates of the other men's vehicles.

Olsen crossed in front of his Chevy into the street. As he grabbed his door handle, he looked down the block. Right at her.

Charlie's pulse spiked. She lowered the camera.

Had the lens reflected the light from a streetlamp and caught his attention?

His gaze was locked on her, eyes narrowing. Letting go of the door handle, he stalked down the street. Headed straight for her.

She tugged on the bill of her cap to hide her face. Cranking the key in the ignition, she fired up the Jeep. Seth took off in a jog. She threw the SUV in reverse and raced backward, swerving around the corner. On the perpendicular block, she whipped the steering wheel, doing a one-eighty, put the gear in drive and sped off. She glanced in the rearview mirror.

Olsen rounded the bend.

Flooring the accelerator, she made a hard right, running a stop sign, tires screeching.

Her heart pounded wildly, adrenaline flaring hot in her system. That was a close call. Too close. She only hoped that Seth hadn't gotten the license plate number.

Charlie made a few more sharp turns and checked to be sure she wasn't followed before slowing down. She stuck to the speed limit, adhering to every traffic rule all the way to Brian's driveway.

Relief poured through Charlie. Not only to have gotten away from Olsen, but to be at Brian's. The knowledge she wouldn't be alone tonight was a comfort.

There was safety in numbers, but more than that, Brian's concern for her was genuine. Exceeded some loyalty to her cousin. He truly was nice.

All the time.

And their chemistry…

The thought of his bed and him in it sounded tempting.

Charlie stuffed the camera in her duffel, uncertain if she'd mention to Brian what had just happened. He'd only berate her and worry. She could do without a lecture.

Drawing a deep breath, she shut her eyes for a moment. All she saw was Seth. The way Olsen had stared at her, seething. Like he wanted to tear through the glass and metal of the car to get to her.

Charlie's heart was still pounding.

Shake it off. Don't let Brian see it.

She hid the camera in her bag and got out. At the door there was a sticky note telling her it was open.

Strange not to ring the bell or knock first without having a key, but Charlie went in and locked the door behind her. Down the hall, the back door to the patio was open. Although the porch light was off, she glimpsed one of the rocking chairs in motion. He must really love it out there.

She set her duffel on one of the stools at the island in the kitchen. On the countertop was a plate of food, steak and veggies, covered with plastic wrap along with another note that read, "In case you're hungry."

His thoughtfulness knew no bounds. Had she known he was going to go out of his way to fix dinner, she would have chosen the home-cooked meal over greasy fast food. She put the plate in the fridge and grabbed the bottle of wine. Turning, she opened a cabinet. Dishes. She tried another one. Glasses. She pulled one down and poured a hefty amount of chardonnay.

She strode down the hall and out onto the covered deck.

He tilted his head to the side, catching her gaze. "Join me," he said, indicating the rocker next to him.

She sat, sipped the cool, crisp wine. Tipping her head back, she stared at the evening sky. An unfamiliar yearning flooded her chest like starlight. For this peacefulness never to end.

For him to kiss her again.

"I was worried," he said, his voice low, soft. "You didn't call to let me know you'd be late. You closed USD more than hour ago."

She stiffened, not accustomed to answering to someone, much less checking in. "Brian, I—"

He took her hand in his, linking their fingers. "I know. Just saying I was concerned. Next time, call, so I don't have to go looking for you. Okay?" His tone was calm, understanding—impossible to balk at.

Lowering her head, she pulled her hand free into her lap. "I don't let people close for a reason. It's not just to protect myself," she said, "but also the few people I have in my life. I keep Rocco at a distance because I don't want my world to taint his. You asked me for full disclosure. I'm willing to give it, but you should know beforehand that it'll compromise you. As a police officer."

Fixing her with a stare, he stopped rocking. "Compromise how?"

She shook her head, exasperated. She wanted his help, not to ruin his career. Dragging him into this was a mistake. One she didn't want him to regret.

He put a hand on her shoulder and squeezed. "Let's start with you telling me what you learned from Rafe Martinez. We'll work our way up to the full disclosure part. Baby steps. Yeah?"

Charlie's stomach flip-flopped. She'd warned him his job could be jeopardized and he was more concerned about her taking baby steps than about protecting himself.

Her style was to rip off the Band-Aid and get it over and done with, but if he wanted to delay the inevitable ugly part, then she'd do it his way.

She sucked in a deep breath. "Rafe told me that he and Haley were only friends. Never anything sexual between them."

"Do you believe him?"

Another sip of wine. "He's gay."

"Oh." Brian nodded. "But he's definitely hiding something."

"Rafe claimed that Seth believed he was having an affair with Haley. Jumped him one night as he was closing the shop. Wore a ski mask and beat him up."

Brian leaned forward, resting his forearms on his thighs. "Why didn't he report it?"

"Too afraid. Seth threatened to kill him if he talked."

"Allegedly," Brian said.

"You still don't think that a cop, one you know, is capable of something like beating up his wife, or her best friend, or murder?"

"That's not what I think."

She waited for him to tell her what was going through his head, but only stared back, cool and collected. "You can't put the assault in an official report. Rafe is worried about it getting back to him."

Brian looked insulted. "Give me some credit," he said. "Listen, Internal Affairs is going to investigate Seth. They're impartial, coming in from Cheyenne. Talk to Rafe again. Let him know. See if he'll speak to them."

"I can try." But she doubted he would be receptive to the idea. She wouldn't be if she was in his position.

"When was the last time he has seen Haley?"

"Not for months. Not since the assault." Poor guy. His story tracked with Seth's history of abuse and violence according to what she'd learned from Haley.

She tipped the glass up to her lips, letting the wine slide down her throat.

"Dead end on who owns the house on Mulberry," he said. When Charlie frowned, he added, "More like a closed door. My friend, Melanie Merritt, is going to help me pry it open."

"The assistant district attorney?" she asked, choking on her wine, and he nodded. "Must be nice to have friends in high places."

A look crossed his face like he wanted to say more but was hesitant.

"I've got two more addresses for you to look into.

One in Centennial and the other in Woods Landing-Jelm."

"Please tell me this doesn't mean that you're still following Seth."

"Then I won't. I'll text you the addresses."

"It's dangerous following him. You need to stop. If he's not on to you now, it's only a matter of time. Then you'll have more to worry about than what happened to Haley," he said, and she shifted her gaze to the sky. "Are you listening to me?"

Sighing, she was annoyed by the parental tone, and the fact he was right. Olsen was on to her because she'd gotten sloppy, ventured too close to the house on Mulberry. Confessing it to Brian, after his little lecture, would only upset him. And worry him.

To her surprise, it was nice having someone concerned about her welfare. "I hear you."

"I checked out Seth. The story of domestic violence."

She perked up in the rocking chair. "And what did you find?"

"Nothing official documented about abuse. Not a single 911 call from Haley. No complaints. No medical history at the hospital to support it either."

"You don't believe me." Charlie's breath caught. "After what I told you, about seeing the bruises myself."

"Haley Olsen never reported any kind of domestic violence. Not at the hospital. Not in a 911 call. Detective Kent Kramer spoke to her family. Not a word to them about it, either. Nothing. While Seth's record is clean. Not a blemish on it."

She couldn't believe what she was hearing.

"Did you know Haley used to be a stripper at the Bare Back?" he asked.

Not until today, but she nodded.

"Rumor is, Haley was cheating on Seth. If not with Rafe, then maybe with someone else. The only report, the only evidence I could find, was about Haley. Taking a baseball bat to Seth's truck."

"What? When?"

"Six months ago. On Valentine's Day no less. Want to guess where?"

No, she didn't.

"In the parking lot of Delgado's. Other cops were there and saw it. The only reason she wasn't arrested is because Seth said it was a personal matter and that he didn't want her charged."

Six months? Valentine's. "I bet she did it because of Rafe. The assault. It happened last February." Maybe that was the final straw. What drove her to USD a few short months later.

"It doesn't matter why. What does matter is that there's evidence, with eyewitnesses on record, of Haley, an alleged abused wife, terrified of her husband, being violent. Being the aggressor. In public. While her demon of a husband defended her. Protected her. Kept her out of jail. The dots don't connect. It's not adding up."

She heaved a breath.

This didn't sit well with her. For one thing, the

night Charlie had talked to Haley about the possibility of fake credentials, starting a new life somewhere else, Haley had been a quivering, frightened victim who'd gone through a box of tissues. The entire time she'd blamed herself for the beatings, worried about what might happen to her if Seth discovered her plan to leave and questioned whether it might be better to stay.

Was it possible that there was another side to Haley, a side Charlie knew nothing about?

She got up, strode to the railing of the deck, leaned on it. "Did you find anything to give you a grain of doubt about him?"

"I did." Brian stood and joined her. "His alibi, being with Detective Colvin, can't be verified. They weren't on duty. No one else saw them together. They weren't caught on traffic cameras, either."

"Then he's not free and clear," she said. "His record might be clean, but maybe it's because he hasn't been caught yet. It doesn't mean his hands aren't dirty."

"You're right. It's not cut-and-dried. There's more to it all, and I'm going to get to the bottom of it."

"You do care about this," she said. "About what happened to Haley."

"Of course, I care. A woman has disappeared. Her husband, a cop, might be responsible. And if not for that, then possibly other illegal things. This matters to me, but you matter more."

She drew in a deep breath, held it, exhaled relief

that Brian wasn't giving up. The part about mattering to him, she was quite sure what to do with it.

Easing in front of her, he closed the gap between them and pinned her with a long, steady look that made her stomach flutter. "I need to know what you're keeping from me. What are you afraid for me to find out?"

"I'm not exactly a model citizen."

"Are we talking dead bodies buried somewhere?" he asked, easy-breezy.

It wasn't as bad as that, still, she grunted her frustration. This was serious. Life-changing. Career-ending. She wished he'd act like it. "What if I told you I had killed someone? What would you do?"

His dark brows knit together. "I'd ask you why you did it."

His reasonable response, the best she could really hope for, didn't make her feel any better.

He gazed down at her calmly. "Stop testing me. Tell me what it is."

She gulped the rest of her wine. Why did he have to push this?

"Hey," he said. "I want you to think of this deck as a safe space. A confessional. You share with me, and I'll never violate your trust."

She frowned at the monumental promise he couldn't possibly keep.

"Give me a chance, Charlie."

"For what, to let me down?"

He cupped her face in his hand and stroked her cheek with his thumb. "Have I disappointed you yet?"

No. He hadn't.

"You're no coward," he said. "This isn't the time to start acting like one."

Now he was testing her. Pushing her. Right out of her cagey comfort zone.

BRIAN WAITED FOR Charlie to respond, bracing himself for… Well, for anything. It was a given that her confession involved an illicit act. But he knew that Charlie wasn't a murderer, despite her earlier question.

He stared into her eyes, willing her to trust him.

Something in her was broken. Leftover from her childhood, haunting her. To ever heal from it, she was going to have to put her faith in someone. He wanted that person to be him.

"I didn't just convince Haley to leave her husband," she said. "I was in the process of helping her do it."

"Helping in what way?"

"New location. New name. New everything. Get her off his radar. Make it so that he could never find her."

She was talking about illegal, fake credentials. "Is this the first time you've done this?"

"What?"

"Make a person vanish by giving them a new life."

"I've been doing it for three years. A handful of clients. Only women and children who were in a violent situation. Never for criminals."

He lowered his hand from her face, his gut tightening. "Do you make the fake IDs?"

It was tough to get credentials that passed scrutiny. Required specialized skills, and while Charlie was talented, he didn't see *forger* fitting into her wheelhouse.

Then again, she was full of surprises.

"I act as a liaison. The middleman so to speak. My client buys it from one of my contacts. But I make nothing from the deal."

Relief trickled through him that Charlie wasn't a forger or personally selling fake credentials. Not that it was good that she was acting as a go-between, but she should have told him this sooner.

"Maybe Haley decided to leave town early," he said. "Staged the scene at her house to implicate Seth as a going away present."

"Why are you so cynical about this?"

He shrugged. Came with the territory of being a detective and working a case.

"In my heart, I think Haley is dead. There was so much blood. Too much." She shook her head. "If she left, where would she go? She doesn't have a new identity yet. None of her credentials are ready. The clients never have any interaction with my contact. Only I do. And that still doesn't explain who shot at me."

Foul play was certainly possible. The blood found at the house matched Haley's DNA. Forensics also detected latent bloodstains and stated that close to two liters of it had been in the house, though, they'd only been able to analyze traces.

But the fact that a body hadn't turned up was nagging him.

"This is a dangerous business you're in," he said. "Not only for you, but more so for your clients. They have no idea what they might be buying with a fake ID. They could be getting a host of issues from credit problems to a criminal history." There was no telling.

"The identities are solid. There's never been a problem."

"How can you put the lives, the futures of these women and their children, into the hands of some shady scumbag hacker that you don't really know?"

Charlie rested her head back against a wood post and lowered her gaze. "But I do know him."

"How well?"

She took a deep breath, released it. "Intimately. Once upon a time."

A cold lance of jealousy stabbed him. "How long ago?" The words came out harsher than he intended.

She looked up at him, surprise flashing in her eyes.

Yeah, he'd finally lost his cool. Over a former lover of hers, who was also a criminal and still embedded in her life.

"We called it quits four years ago," she said.

He swallowed some of his irritation. "Did you love him?"

She shook her head. No hesitation.

It relieved him to know she hadn't given him her heart only for the guy to break it. "Why did you two end things?" Dating a criminal was the polar opposite of a cop. Should've been exactly what she was looking for, the ultimate bad boy.

"You think I have trust issues?" Charlie arched an eyebrow. "Orson kept hacking into my phone and computer. It was a lot to have my boyfriend constantly spying on me."

"Other than that, he was Mr. Right?"

"Hardly." She gave a chuckle devoid of humor. "Orson likes variety. I'm not big on sharing. We weren't together long. But he was willing to help me even after the breakup. For a price. There aren't many women's shelters in the state, much less this area. I only do this for women who believe their lives are in danger and need to relocate permanently."

"What's Orson's last name?" He was going to dig into this guy, unearth every dirty thing he could about him.

She narrowed her eyes. "Asking me to trust you is one thing. Asking me to violate someone else's is another."

He sighed. "You shouldn't use your ex's services anymore. There are better ways to help someone disappear. Legal ways. Get them off the grid. Plant misleading tracks online. Tell them to only take jobs that pay in cash. That kind of life is significantly harder, but safer."

"If you need to arrest me, to protect your job, I understand. All I ask is that you don't stop investigating what happened to Haley."

Arresting her hadn't been a consideration, especially after she had warned him. It became a *don't ask, don't tell* situation. And he'd made the choice to keep asking. "You shared in the Bradshaw confessional. Your secret stays here."

He respected what she tried to do for Haley. How she saved and protected those who needed her. Even if he didn't agree with her methods, which were legally in the gray, he respected *her*.

"Really?" she asked. The disbelief in her voice chafed him.

A little.

He nodded. "You're safe with me." Maybe now she'd start to believe it.

"I doubted it was possible for us to share the same perspective about this." Putting a palm on his chest, she relaxed her body against his. "I guess I did have your brand wrong."

"I think you might be pleasantly surprised at what we share." He ran his hands down her arms, to her waist, and gripped her hips. She was all lean muscle and soft, subtle curves. "At what we will share." He ached to kiss her.

The same thing must've been on her mind because she slid her hands up into his hair and brought his head down for precisely that. It was hungry and demanding as he wrapped his arms around her. Earlier, she'd been hesitant, caught by surprise.

Now she kissed him back like she was as impatient and needy and eager as he was.

She tugged his shirt out of his pants, slipped her hand under and across his skin. One of her lean, toned thighs eased between his.

The kiss deepened, turning heady, and she gave a little moan.

He wanted her in the worst way. Had for a long time. Ever since their chance run-in at the charity gala in Cheyenne. They'd lowered their guards, had drinks, dinner, real conversation. Deeper than casual chitchat. Laughed together. Brian had taken her hand. They'd ventured into the murmuring crowd where the band played something soft and romantic. On the dance floor, he'd pulled Charlie close, slid his hand down the bare expanse of her back, felt her shiver at his touch. Heard her breath catch in her throat. They moved in sync, two pieces of a puzzle that fit. Others dressed in sequins and tuxes eddied and swirled around them. Overhead, hundreds of tiny lights twinkled like stars. He gazed down at Charlie's upturned face. Captivated by her beauty, by her smile, he'd kissed her without thinking, tasting the champagne on her lips. As she opened her mouth, sliding her tongue over his, wrapping her arms around his neck, pressing even closer, he'd thought he could tell where the night might lead.

Then she backed away and bolted. Fled home to Laramie and returned to giving him the cold shoulder.

For them to have a future, they couldn't sleep together like this. Where she'd take him for a test drive and in the morning, dismiss it as a mistake.

He pulled back and met her gaze. "Not tonight." He wasn't going to blow it by being impulsive. "I made up the guest room for you."

"Why?" she purred. "I thought I was welcome between your sheets."

"You are welcome. In my home. And in my bed. But you're not ready for the latter."

She reached down, cupped his groin and massaged the unmistakable hardness of his desire. "It feels like we're both ready to act on all that *chemistry*. How about some sweaty, no-strings attached fun," she said, low and breathy, her fingers stroking him.

He groaned, yearning to have the feel of her touch all over his body, but he eased her hand away. Kissed her knuckles. "That's just it. I want strings and attachment. What I *don't* want is for us to make love, only to have you run afterward, like some skittish wild horse that's been spooked."

Charlie stilled as if stunned, but she didn't wilt. She was silent. Simply stared at him.

The uneasy quiet stretched between them.

"I want more than sex with you," he said, making sure he got through to her. "I want a relationship."

A sad warmth filled her eyes, along with tears. "I have had walls up for more than twenty years, Brian. I'm not sure I'm capable of tearing them down."

"They're not walls. Merely high fences. I'm rather good at jumping over those." He smiled at her. "You just have to let me." He dug in his pocket and pulled out a key. "It's to the front door. You can come and go without needing me to be here."

She took the key from him. Their fingers grazed and she clung to his hand. "What if you're wrong about me? What if I'm…" Her voice trailed off. A tear rolled down her cheek, and she quickly whisked it away.

"I'm not wrong." He caressed her cheek. "And there's no rush. I can wait." No matter how long it took, even though he knew there were no guarantees. "I'm not asking you to give me forever." Not yet anyway. "Only a chance."

Chapter Eight

Tiptoeing down the hall in her running shoes, Charlie did her best not to make a sound. She didn't want to disturb Brian. Truth be told, she was anxious about seeing him this morning. Their conversation last night had been nerve-racking. She hadn't a clue how he'd take the news about her helping victims of domestic violence procure fake credentials.

But he'd taken it in stride, as usual. Brian had seemed more bothered by her continued association with her ex, Orson, than with her illicit activities. She'd never figured him for the jealous type. Or that he'd tolerate her operating in the gray. Or that he'd reject her offer of sex. Something easy. Casual.

She tried to shrug it off. *No big deal.*

But it had been. A huge deal in fact.

Orson never would've turned her down. Not even after they'd broken up. Sometimes he still tried to have an occasional hookup. Her attraction to him hadn't gone away, but she didn't want to be a part of his revolving door of women. Anything physical or romantic with Orson was dead and buried. Never to be resurrected.

But what kind of guy turned down a no-strings attached good time between the sheets?

She crept around the corner into the kitchen and stopped.

Brian sat at the island, wearing his shorts, a T-shirt and running shoes, drinking a glass of water. He must have been silent as a ninja as he'd gotten ready. She would've sworn he was still asleep.

He snapped his gaze up to hers, direct and penetrating.

Heat flooded her cheeks.

Turning to face her fully, he leaned against the counter. He flicked a look over her from head to toe, like he was striking a match against her body.

Something flared under her skin, the warmth in her cheeks spreading lower.

He was the kind of guy who knew exactly what he wanted and wouldn't settle for less. No denying it was a turn-on.

But she hadn't been any more prepared for his blunt declaration than she was for this face-to-face ambush while she was trying to sneak out. She had always been worried about others disappointing her if she got too close. With Brian, for the first time, she was afraid of being the disappointment.

"Figured I'd join you on your jog." He stood, scraping the stool back against the hardwood floor. "If you don't mind the company."

Of course, she minded, and surely he realized it.

Hence the reason for this surprise attack. "Suit your-self." She made a beeline for the door.

"How far are we going?"

She heard the scuff of his sneakers on the floor behind her. "Only three-point-nine miles," she answered, leading the way to the road.

"That's fairly precise."

"Mapped it out on my smartwatch. We're only going to the rifle range and back. I didn't realize you lived quite so close to me."

His arm brushed hers, sparking a tingle in her belly. "Feels good to be close to you."

He wasn't only talking about the proximity of their houses, but if she focused on that, he'd see her blush.

"Let's go." She took off, setting a brisk pace down Rogue Canyon Road.

He maneuvered to the other side of her, putting himself on the outside where any cars would pass. His protective instinct never quit.

Casting a sidelong glance at him, she admired his excellent posture and the fit of his T-shirt stretched taut over his muscles. With his powerful stride and those big hands, he seemed like he knew his way around a woman's body.

He looked at her.

Busted. Caught her ogling.

"Rocco told me that you left your aunt and uncle's house at seventeen. Right after you graduated high school."

"Yeah."

"He said you bounced around a lot. About every two years."

Rocco talked too much. "That's right."

"I had to move a lot, too, with the military. Not by choice. Why so often for you?"

She shrugged. "Thought I wanted the hustle and bustle. Action. Kept trying different places. New York. Los Angeles. Miami. Chicago. Denver." During her time in Colorado, she'd met Orson.

"Is that why you haven't unpacked everything at your house? Too used to leaving?"

"I guess I like mobility." She hadn't really thought about it before. "But the big cities drained me." Inevitably, it felt as if her soul was being sucked dry. "I feel grounded here. Something to the great outdoors. The simplicity." She never thought the wild west, the landscape and cowboys, would be for her. Glancing at Brian with mountains as the backdrop, she was glad to be wrong.

"You've been in Laramie a while. Almost three years."

She nodded. "Uh-huh." Long time for her.

"Think you'll stay?"

What was this, twenty questions? "USD is the closest thing to putting down roots." That was the best, most honest answer she could give.

She picked up speed, determined to nix the conversation.

With their ridiculously fast pace, they made it to the range and back to his house in almost no time.

Once they reached his driveway, she bent over

and clutched her knees, catching her breath. Somewhat recovered, she stood upright. The sun cast sharp shadows over the hillside and mountains. A cool breeze stirred the trees around them.

Charlie closed her eyes, tipping her head back and inhaling a deep breath; the scent of sweet wildflowers hung in the air. "I love this smell. Different in the morning than at night."

When she opened her eyes, she looked at Brian. His back was to her. A sheen of sweat covered his skin, but he wasn't winded, breathing hard like she was.

He spun on his heel, strode up to her and threw his arms around her in a tight hug.

She went rigid, startled by the intimate contact. Then she found herself melting against him, curling her fingers in his damp T-shirt, soaking in his masculine, sweaty scent.

It felt good to be close to him, too. Scary, but good. She could stay like this a while, wrapped in his arms.

He pressed his mouth to her ear, his breath warm on her neck. "We're being watched. When I let you go, look to your two o'clock. Behind the peachleaf willows. There's a car. Black compact SUV."

She swallowed hard, a knot twisting in her gut.

"It wasn't there when I got home last night," he said. "But it's been there since we left."

He let her go and bent down, pretending to adjust his shoelaces.

Charlie couldn't tell a peachleaf willow from a

weeping one, but he'd told her enough to properly orientate her.

Sure enough, behind a cluster of trees was a black car. Through the branches the sun glinted off the windshield.

"Act natural," Brian said. "I'll climb up to the roof. See if I can get a license plate number. Then we'll get ready and leave in separate vehicles. I want you to go someplace well-populated. Maybe Delgado's."

It was close to USD. Busy from the time they opened until closing. Good spot.

"Then we'll see," he said, "which one of us is being followed."

THE EARLY EVENING heat was sweltering even though the sun was low in the sky. Perspiration rolled down Brian's temples, his mind roiling with worry for Charlie. No one had followed him to the sheriff's department, which meant that Charlie was the target.

At the sheriff's, he'd gone to ask the chief deputy if there were any leads on who shot at her. Also, he had them run the license plate number he was able to get while on the roof.

Came up with the oddest result.

"It's showing as blocked," a deputy had said. "Maybe it's a government vehicle. Or possibly an undercover police vehicle. Wouldn't you be able to find out at the LPD?"

So, he'd passed the plate number on to Kent.

Lowering his binoculars, Brian didn't like the looks of the large house sitting at the address in

Woods Landing-Jelm that Charlie had given him. It was on the back side of Jelm Mountain. About three acres bordering what might be state land. No neighbors nearby.

The place had all the telltale signs of being a meth house. Blackened windows. An unusual ventilation system that pumped wisps of smoke through small pipes on the roof. The smell of rotten eggs carried on the breeze. A couple of armed guys out front smoked cigarettes, presumably security. Dead vegetation around the property. Burn pits in the grass.

The house at the other address in Centennial hadn't been quite the same. Protected by armed guards as well, but it had a different feel to it. Maybe it was used for distribution or storage. He hadn't been able to get too close to that location, either. With it being isolated, security could see someone coming from miles away.

Nothing odd about a narcotics detective checking out such a place. In fact, it could be a sign Seth was only doing his job.

But the thought of Charlie being out here, sneaking around this house, made Brian's blood pressure rise. Meth labs, their cooks and users were extremely dangerous and unpredictable.

He hoped like hell that she listened to him and stayed away from Seth. Was she trying to incite him by following him?

She was certainly underestimating him. He wasn't stupid. And if he was guilty of being dirty and harming his wife, then there was no limit as to what he would do to Charlie.

Last night, he felt as though they'd had a breakthrough. She'd opened up, daring to share a dicey truth in spite of the risks. Showed real trust that he thought they could build upon.

This morning, he wasn't so sure. She hadn't been icy. Only quiet. Like she wasn't certain of the way forward. He had a niggling fear in the back of his mind. About Charlie. That she was going to make excuses to him, even to herself, why they couldn't be together. They might not have slept together, but it didn't mean she wouldn't be inclined to run. She'd been doing it for so many years that it was second nature to her.

As long as she understood that following a detective, who might be dirty and might have killed his wife was too dangerous to continue, then the rest was doable. He'd find a way to scale her fences.

Thinking about Seth, he glanced at his watch. Six twenty. He needed to get going. The first football practice of the season was starting in forty minutes.

Brian slid down the hill he was perched on. Dusted himself off and climbed back into his truck. He pulled off onto the road, heading back to Laramie.

In town, he ignored the fast-food signs calling his name. Charlie had *made* breakfast, which consisted of smoothies. Apparently, she wasn't much of a cook. He'd skipped lunch and could have used a burger something fierce. It would be hours before he'd get a chance to grab dinner.

His cell phone vibrated in his pocket. He took it out. Glanced at the screen. It was Kent. He put the call through Bluetooth. "Did you find something?" He'd expect the guy to wait until Monday to check it out.

"Nada. Sorry. I got the same result as the sheriff's department. It's weird. If it's one of ours, I should be able to see it. Unless someone deliberately wanted it hidden. Or it could be some other explanation. Listen, I'm still in the office looking at something. Got a minute?"

He'd been there for hours.

"It's a Saturday," Brian said. "Your day off."

"I've got no life. Sue me." Kent gave a dry chuckle that Brian suspected was hiding a deep layer of grief. "Anyway, I want to run something by you."

"Yeah, sure," Brian said. "What is it?"

"A woman came into the station yesterday, Donna Williams, to file a missing person's report on her son, Theodore. He goes by Teddy."

"Okay. So, what?" Brian turned onto Grand Avenue, going straight to the field where they played. He'd change in the cab of the truck since he'd packed his gear this morning. "I'm not tracking why you're asking me about it."

"Well, Mrs. Williams says the last time she saw her son was on Monday. He checks in with her every couple of days. When she hadn't heard from him, she swung by his place. The mail in his box has been piling up since Tuesday. She thinks that's when he went missing. Haley disappeared on Wednesday."

"You think the two cases are related somehow?"

"It's been bugging me. That's why I stayed at the office. To look at some stats. Guess how many missing persons we have in the state so far this year?"

"I don't know. A hundred?"

"Forty-five. And I'm talking about folks who didn't turn up after a day or two. In the county, eight. In Laramie, three. Two in the last week."

"You've got my attention. You're thinking it's not a coincidence." Sure didn't sound like one.

"Yep. I went back through Haley's file, searching for a connection. Her family mentioned that she's been taking classes at the Underground Self-Defense school on Third Street for a little less than a year," Kent said, and Brian's gut tightened. "Guess where Teddy Williams worked?"

Brian stifled a groan. "As an instructor at USD."

"Bingo. But that was only his part-time job. Want to know where he worked full-time?"

"You've got me hanging in suspense. Where?" Brian asked.

"At Nelson's gun shop," Kent said. "They sell premium muzzle-loading gunpowder. How much you want to bet it's the same brand that was used as the propellant at the Olsens'?"

"I'd venture to guess that'll be a winning bet. But how many other gun shops carry the stuff?"

"I'll find out. I'm going over to Nelson's now to ask some questions. Then I'll hit up USD."

"Don't worry about USD," Brian said. "I'll handle it. I know the owner."

DITCHING HER TAIL hadn't been easy. The one good thing was now she knew what vehicle to be on the lookout for. A Subaru Forester. But she wasn't able to get the license plate.

How long had she been followed?

It burned her to the bone that she hadn't known, and Brian had to be the one to spot the tail.

She lifted the camera and zoomed out for a wide shot of all the men on the field that Seth was stretching alongside. Ten of them. She got close-ups of each and every one.

Two were familiar. The balding guy and the one with dirty blond hair. She'd have to show their pictures to Brian. He might be able to help figure out who they were.

Another truck pulled to the parking lot beside the field. Looked familiar. The door opened and a man jumped out.

Speak of the devil.

Charlie gripped the steering wheel, leaning forward, and stared at Brian.

Smiling, he ran onto the field. Gave a few high-fives, including one to Seth, and started stretching.

What the hell?

For an hour, she sat spellbound and steaming,

watching Brian play football with his buddies. With Seth Olsen.

Bitterness welled inside her. She snapped photos of them, having fun together, huddling, tackling one another, extending a hand and helping each other up from the field. What was next? Having a drink together? Dinner?

The scene nauseated her.

Brian had gone on and on, warning her about following Seth. Was this the reason why? So she wouldn't discover that they were friends?

Why wouldn't he tell her about this…unless he had something to hide? Was he even seriously investigating Seth? Or merely placating her by letting her think that he was?

No wonder he didn't think Seth was guilty.

Brian Bradshaw—too good to be true.

She banged her skull back against the head rest. She had believed all the things he'd said, wanted to believe *in him*.

Whenever they spoke, he really looked at her. Listened to her. As though he could see into her soul. Like he appreciated what made her unique. What a fool she'd been getting sucked in by his niceness, his consideration, his patience, his empathy. His hotness.

His whole brand.

Was any of it real?

The only thing she should have put her faith in was the power of the blue wall. Cops stuck together. The proof was right in front of her, wrapping up their football game.

Brian slung an arm around Seth, clasping his shoulder, like they were close chums. All the guys headed to the parking lot.

A little knife twisted in her chest. He had been holding out on her. Not telling her every little detail was understandable. This was major. Tantamount to lying.

In an hour or two, Seth would probably be at the. The idea of Brian being there with him, and the rest of the fellas, made her stomach turn.

Then it struck her. That's why he had given her a key. So he didn't have to wait at his house for her and was free to hang out with Seth. His good pal. She wanted to spit the disgust from her mouth.

Well, she'd be there, too. It was time she found out what was going on inside that club and why Aubrey had lied to her.

No more lies. She was going to get to the truth.

She backed out of the lot across the street from the field and drove to a salon she'd been to a couple of times. Hair Dreams and Beyond. They specialized in makeovers and wigs.

At the reception counter, she put down her credit card. "I don't have an appointment. But I need someone to make me look totally different. Like a new person. Right now. Whatever the cost, I'll pay double."

The receptionist spun in her chair. "Carey! I've got a client for you. She wants the Lover's Quarrel special, and she's in a rush."

"Let me grab a pop! Send her back."

The receptionist whirled back around. "Go on. Last chair on the right."

Charlie marched back and plopped down in the chair. She dumped her purse on the floor and drummed her fingers on the arm of the chair. And waited.

She remembered she'd told Dustin she would close tonight. Now her plans had changed. Groaning, she dug her phone out of her handbag and called him. "Hey, do we have anyone scheduled for any training sessions tonight?"

"We did. But they called to cancel, and I just finished the last group class of the day."

"And no word from Teddy?"

"Nope."

She shook her head in frustration. "He's been dodging my calls, not picking up." She didn't want to fire the guy in a voice mail, but it was looking like that was what she'd have to do. "Get out of there. Post a note on the website and on the front door. Say that we'll be closing early for the next week." She'd have to call any clients scheduled and apologize for the inconvenience. "Then lock up and skedaddle."

"Okay. Sounds good. Don't forget that I have to leave by four tomorrow. You'll have to close."

"Sure. No problem. I appreciate how flexible you've been."

"Enough to give me a raise?" Dustin asked in a hesitant voice.

Well, she was down a trainer. Why not reward the dependable one. "We'll talk about how much, but yes. You've earned one. Thanks, again." She clicked off.

Finally, someone strutted through the hanging string beaded curtain, holding a can of Coke. "Bonsoir, cherie. My pronouns are they, them and theirs," Carey said, wearing a low cut, formfitting top, slim pants and chunky platform boots. "What can I do for you? Do you want me to transform you into someone else or are you looking to slay, become so drop-dead gorgeous that we call it revenge?"

Deep down, slaying sounded like it'd be satisfying. She was angry enough to spit nails. "I need to look like a different person for a few hours. Nothing permanent. Feel free to wave your wand and add in the gorgeous, too. But I need you do it fast."

"All possible, sugar. Although looking at you, I'm picking up way more spice than sweetness. How do you feel about going to the dark side?"

"Been there and never really left."

Carey chuckled. "I hear that. By the time I'm done, you'll be unrecognizable."

Chapter Nine

After an hour of tackle football, Brian was starving. He'd set a pot of water to boil while he showered. Only bothering to throw on boxer briefs and a pair of jeans, he finished making spaghetti and meatballs.

His preference would have been to wait for Charlie, but she was going to be at USD a while longer and he was hungry enough to eat cardboard.

He scarfed down the food and was wiping up the last of the sauce from his plate with a piece of garlic bread when his front door opened. If he'd known she'd be back early, they could've eaten together.

Swiveling on the stool to face her, he was about to apologize, but a fit of helpless choking stopped him. A stunning raven-haired woman, wearing a tad too much makeup, stalked past him, without a glance in his direction or saying a word.

"Charlie?" It was her…but didn't look anything like her. He was off the stool and hurrying down the hall after her. "What is going on?"

"You don't get to ask me questions anymore." She stormed into the guest room, and he was on her heels.

"Clearly, you're upset about something," he said, keeping his tone calm. "Please tell me what it is."

She grabbed her large travel backpack that could hold a week's worth of clothes and fished around inside.

Up close, he got a better look at her. Thick black eyeliner drawn at an angle gave her sexy cat's eyes. Crimson red lipstick popped against her creamy, porcelain skin. But it was the shoulder-length jet-black hair with cascading waves that he couldn't stop staring at.

Why was she wearing a wig?

Brian caught her arm to stop her from whatever she was doing. "Hey. Talk to me."

Finally, she glanced at him. Her gaze dipped to his bare chest. She faltered a second and then met his eyes. "I don't blame you. It's my own fault. I should've known better than to ever let a cop in my house, much less my life. I don't know what I was thinking." She jerked her arm free of his grasp. "That's the problem. I wasn't thinking. I was an idiot. Lost my head."

Gritting his teeth, he wished they were speaking the same language. He was so confused.

"I know you're afraid of this, Charlie," he said, taking a wild stab in the dark at what the issue could be. "Of having a relationship. But you can't run forever. One day you're going to look around at your life and realize something huge is missing. By then, it might be too late."

She yanked a black lace bra and something else

from the bag. "A relationship?" she scoffed. "You think I'm running from you? That I'm afraid of what? Falling in love? Oh, please." She pulled her T-shirt off over her head, revealing a sports bra and smooth, taut abs.

Lowering his head, he turned away. He'd been dying to get her undressed in a bedroom, but this wasn't how he had envisioned it. "Then why are you angry?"

"I'm not angry. I'm furious," she said, and he could hear her changing clothes. "I can't believe I shared all that personal stuff with you. My past. My pain. That I let you in and put everything on the line. I trusted you. While this entire time, you've been playing me."

"What are you talking about?"

Her high heels clacking against the floor, Charlie prowled around to stare him in the eyes. She'd changed into a low-cut dress that showed off the lace of her bra, exposed her trim, bare thighs and clung to her body like a second skin.

It was so short, was it even a dress?

"You're friends with Seth Olsen," she said through clenched teeth.

Brian swore under his breath. "I told you to stop following him."

"So I wouldn't see you two together, acting like bosom buddies. Go on, deny it. I dare you." She marched out of the room, with her backpack slung over her shoulder. "You're supposed to be investigating him. Not hanging out with him. How could you lie to me?"

The sharp staccato of her heels striking the hardwood rang in his head.

"It was an omission. I never lied to you."

"I'm thirty years old. I've only been close to four people my entire life. My mother. Who was killed in front of me. Rocco and his parents. Even with them, it's easier, safer to hold back."

"Hold what back?"

"Letting it matter. If the disappointment, a lie, some offense mattered too much, it would grind me down until I was nothing. Been there. Disappearing in my grief and my guilt. I can't be nothing ever again."

She took his breath away.

Brian fought to think. To respond.

"I was a victim for most of my life. People pitying me. Making choices for me. Decisions. Pushing the buttons. Manipulating me. All for my own good," she said with such disdain and anger, he could only focus on the underlying pain.

"Is that what you think I'm doing?"

"Isn't that what's happening? How you twisted things," she said, "to make me feel bad about keeping secrets. Unreal."

He was right behind her. "I know how this looks. Give me five minutes to explain."

"Five minutes to reel me back in. I don't think so." She headed for the front door. "There's nothing you could possibly say to change this."

Desperate and at a loss, he said the one thing he could. "Rocco knew."

She stopped.

Glancing over her shoulder, she narrowed her eyes at him, giving him a look that could peel paint from the wall. "Knew what?"

"That I was friendly acquaintances with Seth. About us playing football together. Having drinks on occasion. Sometimes dinner with all the guys. When he called to ask me to help you, I told him. *Full disclosure*. He asked me to keep it from you. Didn't think you'd react well."

In hindsight, Brian should've told her. Not when he first went to her house and was working on gaining her trust, but he should've found the right time. Rather than letting this blindside her.

Dropping her gaze, she pulled something from her pocket and threw it at him.

He caught it.

The key to his house.

"Thanks," she said. "Now I get to be angry at you and my cousin." She opened the door and stormed outside. "How dare the two of you decide what I should and shouldn't know? All in my best interest, right?"

"Where are you going?"

"None of your business!" She threw her backpack into the SUV and slammed the door.

Brian clenched his teeth until his jaw hurt. He tried not to explode. Or to go over and stop her, which would've required physical restraint. She would see it as hostile and then things would really spiral out of control.

"Do us both a favor and stay away from me!" She slid inside the vehicle and took off, tearing out of the driveway.

With Charlie's fixation on Haley, her destination most likely involved Seth and it was only going to lead to pain. For her. Never had he met a woman more prone to hazardous situations. Like danger was drawn to her. Or maybe she went looking for trouble.

Whichever the case, getting close to her meant an endless number of headaches—such as this, when he knew she was putting herself at risk—were in store for him. No amount of reason or persuasion was going to make her veer from a path once she'd started down it.

He ran back into the house and grabbed a shirt, his boots and his gun. If he had any common sense, he should be the one running away from *her*.

But he couldn't do it. Because the problem was, he was into her. Helplessly in too deep to turn back now.

Like hell he was going to stand by and watch her get hurt. The devil himself couldn't stop him from going after her.

SECURITY AT THE DOOR—she remembered his name was Hammer—did a cursory check of Charlie's purse. She'd expected it and had left her SIG in the vehicle. Hammer looked her up and down, and then waved her inside.

"No cover charge for ladies," said the attendant at the register. "Have a good time."

Charlie eased inside the dimly lit gentlemen's club. The place was as she had imagined.

Well-stocked bar. Men seated at tables around the stage that had a couple of mostly naked girls dancing on the poles. Waitresses walked around in outfits that left little to the imagination, taking orders, carrying drinks and food. Other dancers circulating. Some were giving lap dances.

The place reeked of sleazy desperation.

Feeling like a fish out of water, Charlie didn't want it to show. She went to the bar, ordered a rum and Coke. Paid in cash with a generous tip. She didn't intend to drink much, only a sip here and there, in case anyone was watching her. Tonight, she needed all her senses firing at high speed, not dulled by alcohol.

She swept the place with her gaze. Little red lights from security cameras blinked in the corners of the club. Behind the bar was a long mirror. That would enable her to look around and see everyone, much like the bouncers, but subtly.

The night was young. The later it got, the more bodies would funnel inside. The harder it would be to find Seth and see what was going on.

For a minute or two, she watched the ladies onstage strut and dance and spin on the pole all while donning sky-high heels.

Charlie could barely walk in the pair she had on. It was beyond her how those women were able to manage acrobatics in stilts without face-planting.

Her cheeks burned again with renewed anger. The

only reason she'd packed the heels and this dress was because she was staying with Brian. Their night together at the charity gala had been hard to forget. Part of her wanted to re-create it in some way. Maybe they'd have dinner. Light some candles. Instead of wearing her usual garb of a T-shirt, sports bra, workout leggings and sneakers—all of which did not scream come hither—she'd put on something feminine and skimpy.

Charlie huffed a breath. Who was she fooling? Her plan had been to seduce him. Little did she realize how hard that would be.

If only she could reconcile the things about him that didn't make sense. Why not sleep with her when he had the chance if he didn't care about her?

Maybe he was playing both sides. Appeasing her and protecting Seth.

Taking a sip of the drink, she banished Brian Bradshaw, his handsome face and hot bare chest from her thoughts. She looked around the bar in the mirror.

Where was Seth?

His truck was here.

Aubrey came out of a room off to the side, wearing dental floss and heels. She sashayed across the room, wending in between tables, over to a booth in the corner.

From this end of the bar, Charlie couldn't see much. She picked up her glass and moseyed down to the other side. On the way, she watched the girls dancing. She was hoping to blend in. Not act out of the ordinary for a woman in the club alone. Although she was the only one at the moment. After a stripper did an impressive full side split, Charlie raised her drink up to her. The dancer waved in return.

She slid onto a stool and looked up at the mirror.

In the corner booth, Seth sat with two men. One she'd seen before. The guy with wire-rimmed glasses at the gym. The third man wasn't familiar. She would've remembered the long dark hair and the scar on his cheek that ran from his ear to his mouth. His demeanor was a stark contrast to the guy with glasses. Scarface had a certain deadness about the eyes, a readiness to his posture—all that told her to be wary of him. The men weren't really paying attention to any of the girls. Except for Aubrey.

The redhead tried to cozy up to Scarface, but Seth shooed her away.

Charlie slipped her cell phone from her purse. She brought up the camera app. Extending her arms and hoisting the phone high, she smiled, pretending to take a selfie while getting Seth's table into the pics.

With the poor lighting and lack of flash, she wasn't sure if she'd be able to make out their faces in the shots.

A bouncer approached. "Hey, miss, no photographs allowed. It's a misdemeanor to take a pic of a stripper in any state of undress."

She wanted to tell him that no dancers had been in the photo, but she didn't think that'd help her. "I'm sorry," she said, changing her voice, making it more high-pitched. "Silly me." She put the phone back in her purse and sipped the drink.

Aubrey sauntered up to the bar. "Juan, get me my usual. Put it on Seth's tab."

"Sure thing." Juan poured two shots of vodka in a glass with ice. Filled the rest with soda water and added a squeeze of lemon. "Here you go." The bartender handed her the drink and moved down the bar to take another order.

Aubrey gave Charlie the side-eye. "What brings you in tonight?"

"You do."

"Is that right?" Aubrey asked, glancing around. "You got a boyfriend or husband here with you?"

"Nope." Charlie shook her head. "All by my lonesome. Want to keep me company?"

Aubrey smiled and stepped closer. "We don't get many ladies in here alone. With their fella, sure. In a big gaggle wearing veils and plastic penises on their heads, sure. But alone?" The woman scrutinized her under a laser-eyed gaze. "Not so much."

Possible that was true around here. But Charlie was ready with a story. A toss-up between her being into girls herself. Or she was a stripper at a club in Cheyenne who was scoping out a new place to work.

Since she had the woman that she needed to speak with in front of her, there was no need to play games. "You lied to me about spying for Haley when we spoke in the alley by the dumpster. I want to know why."

Aubrey reeled back. Her eyes narrowed to slits. Then she leaned in. "Charlie?" Panic flashed across her face. "You can't be in here."

"Why did you lie to me? I know you were spying on Seth for Haley."

"You don't know what you're talking about." Aubrey glared at her and lowered her voice. "Get out of here."

"I'm not leaving just yet. Not until you tell me who is sitting at the table with Seth and what they're discussing."

"You were taking pictures of them, weren't you? First time I've seen a woman on her own in here snapping a selfie." Aubrey took a gulp of her drink. "Do you have a death wish, lady? Seth has the instincts of a cobra. He will strike first at any threat, and something has already got him paranoid."

"What's he up to at that table?" Charlie asked. "What's he doing in here every day?"

Aubrey laughed, but the sound was grating. "Business. As usual."

"What kind?"

"The illegal kind. Now you need to get gone," Aubrey said, pointing a finger in her face.

"Why did you lie to me?" Haley was her friend. The stripper didn't have to talk to Charlie, but she'd volunteered. Only to spew half-truths.

The redhead heaved a breath. "Because unlike you, I don't want to die. I hope nothing has happened to Haley, and if it has, then I want that bastard to pay for it. But I've also got to protect myself." She chugged her drink. Slammed the glass on the bar with a clink. "You've got get out of here." Aubrey moved to leave.

Charlie hopped up in front of her. "What kind of business?" she demanded. "Give me something."

"I can't."

"If you don't, I'll keep popping up. Pushing and poking. I'll become your worst nightmare. That's a promise until you tell me."

"Drugs," Aubrey snapped in a harsh whisper. "Prostitution. Money laundering. Take your pick. All right."

"Did Haley know?"

"Yeah. Of course." Aubrey looked over Charlie's shoulder. Her eyes grew wide. "Time for you to get the hell out of here. Use the exit at the rear. Don't come back again." The redhead scurried off, disappearing behind a door marked Employees Only.

Charlie glanced at the booth in the corner.

Empty.

She headed for the front of the club.

Wire-rimmed glasses guy hurried through the doors after someone else. Seth lingered near the entrance, talking to one of the bouncers. He pointed at Charlie. The bouncer nodded as they spoke.

She swore under her breath.

Spinning on her heel, she hustled for the exit at the rear. Her heart pounded, thrumming against her rib cage. She pushed the door open and stumbled into the alley. To the right and around the corner led to the parking lot at the entrance, where Dustin's SUV was parked.

She click-clacked down the alley. Too bad she

hadn't been wearing sneakers. The hairs at the back of her neck twitched to life. She stopped. Listened.

Nothing. No movement. No sound.

She crept to the end of the building and turned the corner.

A dark figure loomed, standing between her and the parking lot. Lean and wiry. Long black hair. He stepped into the light. Jagged scar on his cheek.

Oh, hell.

Chapter Ten

Her gaze clashed with a cold, black stare. There was a second of something close to recognition, even though she had never seen this man before tonight. She knew a predator when she saw one.

Time slowed. Charlie edged backward, clutching her purse. Wishing she had her SIG.

Her brain screamed at her to run, run. *Run!*

Charlie's heart raced, but her feet felt mired in quicksand as she turned and fled. A scrape of leather on pavement behind her, the man closing in. She heard him as much as sensed him.

Adrenaline overcame the initial jolt of fear. She darted to the side. Barely missed the hand that clawed out to grab her.

But he was fast. Much faster than her in those clumsy, loud heels. Fear flooded her veins. Maybe if she made it back to the rear door, she could—

He snatched a hold of her hair—the long tresses secured by well-placed bobby pins—and yanked her backward. Pain pulsed over her scalp, wrenching a cry from her lips.

Not panicking was the most important thing. That's what she taught her clients. She had to get him off. Had to free herself.

Dropping her purse, she pulled out the pins from the front. The force of his grasp ripped the wig from her head. She stumbled at the sudden release. Floundered to find her footing.

A kick sent her reeling into a wall. Her bare shoulder and leg scrubbed against brick, her skin burning from the scrapes.

He swooped in. Clamped a hand around her upper arm and whipped her around. "You're coming with me," he growled at her, but Charlie knew that leaving with an assailant never boded well.

Ninety-five percent of the time if the woman complied, she was dead.

He reached into his jacket pocket.

She didn't wait to see for what. But she imagined a gun in a shoulder holster. Instead, she slammed the sharp point of her heel down onto his foot. He grunted in pain. Driving her knee up into his groin, she shoved him away as he doubled over. His hand fell from his jacket, and she glimpsed the shoulder rig.

If he pulled the gun, running wouldn't save her. It would only get her a bullet in the back or worse, in her head.

She stood her ground but didn't wait to strike again. Size didn't matter in a fight. As a woman, she was never going to get attacked by someone smaller or weaker. It boiled down to thinking outside the box, focusing and moving quicker than her opponent.

Scarface recovered, standing upright when she planted one foot—as best she could in the teeter-totter heels—and pivoted, swinging her elbow up and around. She used the added rotation to drive it hard into the side of the guy's head. If she had attempted to throw a punch that hard, she'd have broken her hand. But her elbow barely felt it.

The guy staggered. But this wasn't his first rodeo being hit in the head. Still off-balance and blinking from the blow, he reached under his jacket again. Charlie grabbed his wrist, holding it inside the jacket so he couldn't pull the weapon from the holster. He was strong, had lots of lean muscle. She rammed her heel onto his foot once more and threw a punch. But he jerked sideways, and she just missed his solar plexus. Had the blow struck where she had aimed, it would have immobilized him, giving her enough time to get away.

He flung her off him and slammed his fist into her gut. A cry crawled up her throat, but she could barely breathe, much less scream. Scarface drew a gun with an attached sound suppressor.

Not something you saw every day.

"We're going to go for a drive," he said, and this time she picked up on his slight accent, "and have a little chat."

The rear door to the club flew open with a clang as it banged on the wall. A blond guy in jeans and a button-down lurched out. "Is this the bathroom?" he asked, tottering deeper into the alley.

A drunk.

"Go back inside," Scarface said, waving his gun at him. "This isn't the toilet."

Dread ricocheted through her. Her lungs squeezed. While there was a witness, she scooted to the side, trying to ease away, but Scarface blocked her path. All he had to do was redirect the aim of the muzzle at her.

If the drunk left, Scarface was going to drag her away somewhere, question her and then kill her. She sensed it in her bones.

"What? Really?" the drunk said. "Man, I can't hold it." The blond guy stumbled over to the opposite brick wall and unzipped his pants. "Give me a minute." He shoved his hand in his pants, jiggled around. Then he spun around, drawing a gun. Something small, microcompact. "Police! Drop your weapon!"

For a dazed second, she stared at the blond man in shock. His feet were spread wide, his gun raised.

Scarface squeezed the trigger. Bullets bit into the brick facade near the blond's head as the other guy bolted around the corner. Footsteps thundered around the side of the building toward the front of the club.

Charlie swayed, balancing on her heels.

The blond turned to her with the gun in his hand and said, "I'm DCI Logan Powell. Give me your car keys."

A wave of confusion gripped her. *Powell*. Same surname as the chief deputy. "What?"

"Charlie Sharp, I'm a cop, who just saved your life. Give me your keys. I need to get you to safety."

She searched the ground. Found her purse. Fumbled for the keys. Hurled them.

"Here." He tossed her a key fob. "Go that way." He pointed to the opposite side of the alley. "There's a roadhouse on the other end," he said, and she knew the place. "You'll find my vehicle there. Meet me in the parking lot of the big-box store on Grand. Back end of the lot adjacent to the avenue. I'll explain there." He turned and took off in the direction Scarface had gone.

Charlie raced down the lane, hating the raucous clatter of her heels, but there was no way she was going barefoot.

The alley opened to A.J.'s Roadhouse. A rough, rowdy place. Lots of bikers. Brawls often broke out. All to be expected in this seedy part of town.

The guy hadn't told her what he was driving. She scanned the lot and pressed on the key fob.

Lights flashed at her nine o'clock. She wobbled over to a crossover SUV. A Subaru Forester. Was it the same one that had been following her?

She got in and sped off.

By the time she drove into the back end of the parking lot of the big-box store off Grand Avenue, she was still shaking.

The area was well-lit and buzzing with activity. Other cars were parked nearby. Shoppers moving back and forth between the store and the lot.

She plucked the rest of the bobby pins out and removed the wig cap. Her thoughts whirled in her head. She replayed the incident in the alley and shuddered.

Dustin's SUV pulled up alongside the Subaru. The blond hopped out, came around the side and climbed into his vehicle.

"Before you utter a word," she said, "I need to see some ID."

He pointed to the glove compartment. Reached for it slowly and pulled out a leather folio. He flipped it open.

Charlie eyed the photograph, along with the badge, the name and title beneath it: Logan Powell. Wyoming State Attorney General's Office, Division of Criminal Investigation.

"Okay?" he asked.

"Powell. Are you related to the chief deputy. Holden. And the fire marshal." She couldn't remember his name.

Staring at this man up close, she already knew the answer. The resemblance to Holden was unmistakable. Same golden blond hair and bright blue, earnest eyes.

"Sawyer. Yeah. They're my brothers." For a moment, he just looked at her.

"You've been following me?" she asked.

"I was following the guy you've been tracking. Seth Olsen. I was sent here to investigate him. Then last night, I followed him following you."

She shook her head. "No. I made sure I lost him."

"He made sure you thought you lost him. Olsen is a seasoned detective who has been at this a long time. It's his job to follow people without them knowing."

Brian had warned her. She should've listened to him. He was only trying to keep her safe. Maybe shouldn't have at the very least let him explain.

A shadow swept up to the window on the passenger's side. Rapped on the glass with a gun. Bent down and peered in the car. "Can I join the party?" Brian asked.

SITTING IN THE back seat of the Subaru, Brian gritted his teeth as Charlie got him up to speed about the attack in the alley and this guy's intervention. He hated that he hadn't been the one to protect her, but the only thing that mattered was her safety.

Brian figured that if he had waltzed into the strip club, he would've upset Charlie further, blowing her disguise—moot point now—and only sabotaged her efforts with his presence.

The second he saw that slick guy with the scar racing around to the back of the club, with Seth standing near the entrance, he knew something was up, but prayed he'd spot Charlie leaving any second.

What he hadn't expected was to see some strange man getting in the vehicle that Charlie had been driving.

"I need to see your badge," Brian said.

With a sigh, the guy handed him the folio. Brian scrutinized it. Definitely real.

Brian gave it back. "How many of you Powell boys are there?" He'd gone to high school with at least two of them. But they hadn't run in the same circles.

"Five."

That's a lot of Powells. "Who sent you to investigate?"

"LPD chief. Willa Nelson. She made a formal request with the state attorney general's office," Logan said.

"To look into the disappearance of Haley Olsen?" Charlie asked.

"No. I'm afraid not."

"Then why are you here?" Brian asked.

"To look into police corruption."

"Maybe you shouldn't answer any more of his questions." Charlie folded her arms. "It's one thing to play me, Brian, but if your conflict of interest by being buddies with Seth Olsen is going to compromise this—"

"Now, hold on a minute. I'm going to say this one last time, and I want you to hear me. I am *not* friends with Seth."

"I've got pictures that say otherwise," she told him.

"I was trying to use the football game to my advantage. Hoping he might let something slip. Sometimes it's the smallest detail that can make the biggest difference. For instance, the way he talks about Haley. Never past tense. Like he doesn't think she's dead. Or he wasn't the one who killed her."

"So, you're back to sticking up for him?" she asked, meeting his gaze in the rearview mirror.

Brian leaned forward and rested his arm on the seat. "I'm not. I swear it. I'm talking to you like a detective investigating. I don't think he blew up his own house. But I do think he and Colvin are lying about the alibi. Among other things." His gaze dropped to her shoulder. "You're bleeding."

She glanced at the scrape. "It stings, but I'll live."

"Can I interject, or should I give you two a minute alone?" Logan asked.

Brian clenched his jaw that this guy was here while he needed to sort things with Charlie.

"We've been digging into Detective Olsen for some time," Logan said. "I can assure you that Detective Bradshaw has been nowhere near him or his associates. From what we've observed, they're not even buddies. And Bradshaw isn't one of the cops being investigated or even under suspicion. In fact, he's one of the few that we believe for certain are clean. I hope that resolves the disagreement so that we can focus on business."

Chewing on her bottom lip, she met Brian's gaze again. Her features softer, her posture less defensive.

Maybe Logan Powell wasn't so bad after all. "You said *we've been digging*. Who is *we*?" he asked the DCI agent.

"A special task force. That's all I'm at liberty to say."

This was big. So much bigger than Brian had suspected.

"Once Haley disappeared," Logan said, "I was planning to come speak with you, Charlie, but things have been moving fast. A lot of different pieces and players on the board. Then Detective Olsen followed you and this opportunity presented itself."

Brian went rigid. The dread over Charlie's safety that had been dogging him since someone shot at her now intensified. "Say that again? Seth has been following *her*? For how long?"

"Last night he caught her surveilling him," Logan said. "I followed him following her. I kept watch in case he tried something."

Brian shot her a withering look.

Charlie lowered her head. "Please don't say something as cliché as *I told you so*."

His blood burned to say a heck of a lot more than that.

"Do you two need a minute?" Logan asked.

Brian nodded. "Yes."

Charlie shook her head. "No. Why did you want to speak with me?"

"I was hoping you could help us find Haley Olsen."

"Ask her husband," Charlie said. "I can't help you. Maybe you should try dragging the lake behind the house that blew up."

"We did."

News to Brian.

Charlie blinked at Logan, then she shifted her gaze to Brian.

He shook his head. "I didn't know."

"No one at LPD does. That's the point. We've been investigating under Detective Olsen's radar." He looked at Brian. "Not a word of this to anyone else in the department, okay?"

"Yeah. Sure."

"If you think Haley is alive," Charlie said, "why are you trying to find her?"

The dots were finally connecting for Brian. "You approached her, didn't you? Asked her to work with you on nailing Seth."

"You wanted her to testify against him?" Alarm rang in Charlie's voice.

"Not with spousal privilege," Brian said. "She wouldn't have been able to testify against her husband."

Charlie shook her head. "Then I don't understand how you expected her to help nail him."

"Haley was aware of her husband's activities. We needed her to wear a wire. To get him talking about the operation."

Not hiding the outrage from her face, Charlie glowered at the agent. "And jeopardize her life in the process."

Logan frowned. "The harsh reality is that her life was already at risk."

"She would've understood the danger," Charlie said. "There's no way she would've simply agreed."

"She didn't. We had to apply some pressure."

"Maybe too much pressure," Brian said. "Maybe you scared her off. When did you first approach her?"

"Back in May."

Sighing, Charlie slumped in the seat like she was deflating. "That's when she first came to USD. You, your task force, is the reason she came to me to disappear."

Logan nodded. "Unfortunately, you're probably right."

"I believe Seth got wind of it somehow and killed her for it," Charlie said. "You should be investigating him for murder."

"We are." Logan glanced between them. "But not Haley's."

"Then whose?" Charlie asked in disbelief.

"Teddy Williams?" Brian ventured a guess, and Logan nodded again.

She gasped. "What? Teddy is dead?"

"I found out earlier today that he's been missing since Monday or Tuesday," Brian said. "Detective Kramer, my partner on this, made a connection between him and Haley through USD."

"We don't know for certain that he's dead. But he vanished before Haley, and we have reason to suspect foul play."

"Why would Seth kill him?" Charlie asked.

"Haley and Teddy were having an affair," Logan said. "Someone on the task force threatened to expose her if she didn't come through with assisting us in the case. I disagreed with the method. Coercion rarely works."

"Oh, my God." Charlie shrank back. "Did some reckless, overzealous cop on your team leak it to Olsen?"

"I don't think so."

Brian didn't like the lack of conviction in Logan's voice. If someone on Logan's task force had, he wouldn't admit it to Charlie. Not when his apparent mission was to recruit her.

"If you were going to help Haley disappear," Logan said, "maybe you know how to find her. Start looking at this like she's alive. Think it through." Logan handed her a business card along with keys. "If you come up with something, if you're able to find her, will you call me?"

Charlie didn't respond. She snatched both from him and hopped out. "If Haley is dead, then this is on you and your task force," she said, before slamming the door.

Chapter Eleven

Emotions tangled in a knot in the pit of her stomach.

"We need to talk," Brian said behind her as she walked around to the SUV.

Anger simmered over how the boys, Brian and Rocco, had decided to hide things from her. *Poor, fragile Charlie.* While a warmth she'd never known filled her at knowing that Brian hadn't given up on her. That he'd followed her. Because he cared.

She pressed the button on the fob, unlocking the door, and reached for the handle.

But he put a palm to the door, stopping her from opening it. "Are you going to ignore me?"

"What is there to say?"

"Unbelievable. How about giving me an apology for hurling accusations and not giving me *five minutes* to explain?"

Brian had no idea the power he wielded—the things he stirred inside her. He'd slipped beneath the surface, had her revealing secrets, talking about her past. Stuff she never discussed. Not with Rocco. Not with Orson. Not anyone. Brian managed to break past the defenses she'd taken so long to build and made her feel raw. Exposed. Stripped utterly bare around him.

It was liberating and terrifying and beautiful.

She couldn't imagine what he would've accomplished in five minutes, especially if he'd touched her. "I needed distance. Time to think about it." She hated that she'd doubted Brian, and that he'd given her reason to. Because to her amazement she liked trusting him. "I'm not going to apologize for wanting space. Or for being relieved that I was wrong about you."

"Wow. I'll unpack that dodgy double-talk to evade an actual apology later. For now, you're clearly still upset with me. Why?"

"Your omission feels like a lie. A double standard. You hid it from me." She glared up at him. "Decided with Rocco that I was incapable of handling it."

"You're right. I'm sorry. I should have told you." He eased closer, close enough for her to feel his body heat, his breath across her skin. "But don't lecture me on double standards and hiding things. Not after I had to hear from another man what you've been up to." And then his hand was in her hair.

Her breath caught. Every muscle tensed as he crushed his mouth to hers. Hot and deep, full of wanting and need, he kissed her. She pressed against his hard body, sinking into it, savoring his touch. His mouth was warm and firm. The scrape of his stubble on her skin lit up her nerve endings. He tasted good. Felt even better.

His hands traveled over her body, lingering on her curves. The fluttering inside her went wild. Warmth simmered until she wanted to drag him into the car and strip off his clothes. Chuck hers as well.

"Come home with me," he whispered against her mouth. His voice urgent, almost desperate. The suggestion delivered with a meaningful look.

Her heart threatened to beat out of her chest, reflexes struggling with her fight or flight response.

Then she remembered that there were more pleasurable options. She kissed him again, a soft brush of her lips, not wanting to stop. Not wanting to think. Or speak.

She nodded okay.

He pulled the key from the door, took her hand and popped the trunk. "Let's ride together. We can pick up the SUV in the morning." He grabbed her backpack and put it on his shoulder.

They got into his truck and headed to his house.

In the dark quiet of the truck cabin, he asked, "Is there anything else that you're hiding?" His tone gentle, teasing.

"I've been taking pictures of Seth and everyone I've seen with him. Including in the club." She opened her purse. Looked at the pictures on her phone. "It was so dark in there. You can't see the guy with the scar. The one who attacked me in the alley. But I have better photos of the man with glasses on my camera."

He shot her a heated look. "What am I missing?

What possessed you to go to the Bare Back? Why would that guy attack you?"

"It's a long story, but a stripper who works there, Aubrey, she led me to Rafe. But she lied about not helping Haley spy on Seth. I went back to pin her down and get the truth. Find out what Seth is up to. Turns out it's drugs, money laundering and prostitution."

"Hold on. This Aubrey was working with Haley to do what? Collect evidence?"

She shrugged. "I'm not sure. Aubrey wasn't completely honest. Considering everything I've learned over the past few days, it's obvious that neither was Haley. I think she manipulated me into her helping get the fake credentials. But if she's alive and fled, why wouldn't she wait for the new ID?"

"Maybe it's got to do with Teddy. If Seth did kill him, that might have been enough to push her over the edge. Drive her to do something rash."

"But she can't run far or for long without credentials. Or money. Or the place I was going to set up for her in Idaho." She'd worked out a lease with someone who would accept cash and not run a background check.

"Why there and not halfway across the country? Say Georgia? Alabama?"

"Her mom is sick, and she didn't want to go too far. Even though I warned that she wouldn't be able come back and check on her."

"You've learned a lot," Brian said, pulling into

his driveway. "Any reason you didn't share all this with Powell?"

"You mean about Aubrey and possible evidence?"

"Yeah."

They got out and he carried her backpack and duffel bag inside.

"Haley was either killed or put under so much pressure that she bolted prematurely. I wanted to think before offering up another sacrificial lamb. It's a big decision." Meddling with someone's life.

He locked the door. "If she's on the run, any idea where she'd go?"

"No, but…" An idea came to her.

"What is it?"

"I don't know where she'd go, but I might know how to find her." She dug inside her backpack and whipped out her flip phone.

Brian eyed it. "Is that your burner?"

"Same kind I gave to Haley." Not that it did her any good. She flipped it open.

"Who are you calling?"

She swallowed hard. "Orson."

He looked surprised. Then cautious. "Why?"

"He's the best at what he does. Genius level IQ. Hacked into some government agency when he was only fourteen." She stopped herself from saying more when Brian frowned, twisting his mouth like he tasted something sour.

"A real wunderkind," he grumbled.

On the phone, she pressed and held down the number one, putting the call through.

"You've got him on speed dial? As your first option?" He mumbled something and raked a hand through his hair.

She pressed the phone to her ear. The line rang. And rang. It wasn't like Orson carried the burner around with him. It was probably tucked in a drawer.

"Put it on speaker," Brian said.

She tensed. "Why?"

"Because I'm asking."

She'd asked him to prove that she could trust him. Over and over. And he had. Until the football hiccup, which turned out to be a misunderstanding that he'd wanted to explain. She stared in his eyes and realized she needed to show him that he could trust her, too.

With a nod, she hit the speaker button right as Orson answered.

"Hey, sweet lips." His voice was deep and sultry, warm as a summer night.

Her cheeks flushed and Brian scowled.

"I told you not to call me that," she snapped.

Orson chuckled, the sound reverberating in her belly. "Sorry. It's fun getting a rise out of you. Hey, at least I didn't call you sweet p—"

"I need a favor," she said, cutting him off.

"Of course, you do. It's the only reason you ever call. What is it this time?" Orson asked.

"My latest client, Haley Olsen. She really has disappeared. Possibly. I need you to help me find her if she's still alive."

"I'm listening."

She briefly recounted what happened the night Haley vanished.

"Sounds gnarly. That was Wednesday night?" Orson asked.

"Yes. So, look for someone who has been paying for a hotel in cash since then. Say a sixty-mile radius from here." Haley was worried sick about her mom. She wouldn't want to go far. Especially if she was trying to keep tabs on what was happening back here in Laramie.

Brian shook his head and extended his hands, like he was widening a circle.

"On second thought," she said, "double it. Make it a hundred and twenty miles."

Brian nodded.

"I can use my facial recognition program if you want," Orson said.

Her heart leaped. "Yes. That would be perfect."

"For a price."

He'd never charged her before.

"How much?" she asked. What she was asking for would come with a hefty price tag.

"I don't want your money," he said, sounding insulted. "Come to Denver. Spend a week with me. I miss you."

Sucking in a breath, Charlie turned her back to Brian. For too long, she had allowed this flirtatious banter that skirted a thin line. "You don't miss me. You miss the idea of me. You miss having dinner with someone and a person in your bed who actually knows you." A woman who recognized how special he was, what he was capable of. His brilliance. His drive. His staggering loyalty. He might not have been faithful as a boyfriend, but he was a diehard friend that she could count on in a pinch. "But mostly, you miss the pretense of a relationship. Not me."

They never talked when they were together. Not the way she did with Brian about things that mattered. Orson had never asked her questions, forcing her out of her comfort zone. He preferred to learn about people on the computer. And he certainly never admitted that he cared about her.

Silence stretched, seconds bleeding into a full minute, until it unnerved her. "Orson?"

He sighed. "I hate it when you're right. I guess I just regret the way it ended. You didn't deserve that."

Finding another woman in the bed that they had shared? No. She didn't.

"No regrets. Water under the bridge." Everything worked out the way it was supposed to. She never loved him. Nor him her. Two lost souls who had passed time together. She'd forgiven him ages ago for being disrespectful. It was ancient history now. "Hey, being right doesn't mean I'm smarter."

"I take a strange comfort in that," he said, and she could hear the smile in his voice. "I'll call you when I have something. Keep the phone handy."

The line disconnected.

She exhaled a slow breath of relief, shoved phone in her duffel and faced Brian.

He took her hands in his, and she realized they were shaking.

"Thank you, for trusting me," he said.

"Two-way street. Right?"

A smile tugged at his delicious mouth. God, he was gorgeous.

"Let's get those scrapes cleaned up."

"I think you were a medic in a previous life."

He laughed and led her through the house to his bedroom. She hadn't gotten a good look at it before.

The room was simple, understated, yet tasteful. A deep navy color on the walls. King size bed that took up most of the room. Chic curtains. The duvet looked like it belonged in a swanky hotel. A couple of nightstands with stylish lamps. A photograph of what she presumed was his parents on the dresser.

He sat her down on the bed. "Give me a second." He ducked into the en suite. Came back carrying a large red case that had a white cross on it.

"You brought me in here to flaunt all your medical supplies, didn't you?"

His smile deepened. He unzipped the kit and then she was really impressed. It was the best first-aid kit on the planet. He even the supplies to do sutures. *Show-off.*

He started with cleaning the bruise on her knee.

"Lucky me to have a once-upon-a-time Boy Scout tending to me again," she said, appreciative of his gentle touch.

"Nice to hear that said with affection." He blew on the scrape. Moved to her shoulder and did the same. His gaze raked over her. Not only like he wanted her, but as though she was precious. Valued. Appreciated in return.

Her fear. Her walls…her fences. All the time she'd

spent protecting herself from getting too attached. From being hurt. None of it mattered.

Not in this sweet, safe space that she'd found here with him. She slid her hand into his hair and brought his mouth to hers. The kiss was soft and warm.

"I want to show you something," he said, but hesitated.

"Go on." She nudged him.

He opened a tiny little chest on the nightstand, designed to hold small knickknacks. He pulled something out and opened his palm.

Curious, Charlie stared down at the simple pearl in his hand. "What is that?"

"The night of charity gala for the women's shelter in Cheyenne, you lost an earring."

She'd never had her ears pierced and had worn clip-ons. "The clasp broke." Her gaze dipped back down. "That's the earring? You found it?"

"After you had abandoned me on the dance floor, I came across it. I'd intended to give it back to you. So you could have it fixed."

She reached for it, but he closed his fingers around the pearl.

"My first lie to you." He chuckled to himself. "And my last. I never intended to give it back."

"Got a thing for pearls?" she teased.

"More like for diamonds in the rough. Forged under pressure," he said, and something in her swooned. "This was the closest I could get. I take it out every night. Look at it. Feel it between my fingers. Think of you."

Her gaze went back to his. A sweet warmth coursed through her. Sweeter yet was that she saw he was embarrassed. "That's borderline weird," she said.

"You're being nice. I'm sure it sounds completely weird."

Who was she to judge?

He put the pearl back in the chest, shut it and rose, holding the first-aid kit.

She stood, stopping him with a hand on his chest. "It's also really romantic." In a weird way that she adored.

The night of the gala had been magical for her. Because of him. Running into him when she'd been alone and feeling a bit lost, uncomfortable. Talking to him. Dinner and dancing. Those smooth moves of his. That kiss.

All with him.

It was like Cupid had aimed, released his arrow. And she'd mistaken it for an assassination attempt by the gods.

"I meant what I said last night," he said, his gaze caressing her face the way she longed for his hand to.

"I know." She lifted onto the balls of her feet, still wearing those treacherous heels. And captured his mouth with hers.

Her arms went around his neck, fingers diving into his lush hair. Their bodies slammed together, hers vibrating as the kiss grew rough, nearly brutal with a wild recklessness. His mouth was hot, this time possessive, and she welcomed it. The shock of it sent flares rippling straight to her center.

And the warrior, the survivor in her who had been fighting for so long, so hard, shattered into a thousand pieces. The pain, the loss, the guilt, the anger she'd lived with every single day melted away. Like ashes in rain.

She loved his hair, thick and silky. His mouth. The way he kissed her. She loved his rough hands on her skin, his warm palms pulling her closer.

Desire pooled inside her as his lips moved over hers, kissing down her neck. She rocked her hips against him, aching to get as close as possible.

Pushing him down onto the bed, she straddled him. Kissed him harder, desperation sliding into every stroke of her tongue. His hand slid up, cupping her breast. The other was on her hip. He adjusted their bodies until she was nestled right on top of the rock-hard bulge in his jeans. For too long, she'd been avoiding and wanting this man. Every nerve in her body was alive with the anticipation of spending the next few hours naked with him.

She needed him.

"I want you," she said, the breath shuddering in her lungs as she rocked her hips on him.

"But I need more than the just physical."

Sex, when she chose to have it, was on her terms, always quick and satisfying a basic need. Even with Orson.

Maybe that's why he needed variety. Because she hadn't been willing to do tricks. Perform like a circus act.

But with Brian, there was a tangling of emotions.

A war on her instincts. A battering of expectations. He wasn't looking for entertainment, some carnal thrill.

He wanted to go deeper. To connect by making love.

Another first for her.

"I know," she whispered, nibbling at his mouth, craving all of him. She had no idea that being vulnerable could make her happy. But it did. "I understand."

Making love to him would be taking a giant leap of faith…that he wouldn't break her heart.

But she wasn't blindly jumping in. Her eyes were wide open. And she saw Brian for who he was. A good, strong man. With a kind heart. Not perfect Captain America, but fallible. A guy who could take a licking and keep on ticking.

"What are you saying?" he asked, with a baffled look, cradling her face in his hands.

"I'm saying yes." She was giving him a chance. "Don't blow it."

Chapter Twelve

Driving into town, Brian checked the rearview mirror again. No one had parked near his house, and with the few cars on this stretch of the road, he was certain they weren't being followed.

He reached out and took Charlie's hand. She beamed at him.

"You're beautiful," he said. "Even prettier without the makeup."

She moved her hand from his palm to his thigh and stroked his leg. "Flattery will get you everywhere."

"I'm serious." He glanced over at her. "Did you do something different to your eyebrows?"

"Oh, Carey, *my stylist*, did. Altered the shape to give my face a different look. Subtle, but effective. Do you like it?"

He nodded his approval.

Smiling, she put her head back against the seat and gazed out the window.

After a while, he said, "Penny for your thoughts."

She shrugged. "I'm just happy. Feel like a weight has been lifted." Her smile spread wider. "And I can't stop thinking about last night. Or this morning. I was right about you." She stroked his leg again. "You do know your way around a woman's body. I'm glad your brand isn't Captain America. I don't think he would've been capable of all the dirty, delicious things you did to me."

He chuckled. The night had been incredible. The intensity. The passion. Her guard had lowered and hadn't returned.

This morning had been different when they'd made love again. Sweet. Tender. But no less intense. He'd held her in his arms. Snuggled close, he'd loved the feel of her thigh nestled between his. Her breasts pressed against his chest. The way she kissed up his neck to his jaw. And made them run too late for him to cook breakfast. They'd barely had enough time to shower and grab coffee.

But it was worth it.

He stopped alongside Dustin's Jeep in the big-box store parking lot. "Are you going to get your Hellcat back?"

"If Dustin is willing to give her back that is."

He leaned over and kissed her. "Still want full disclosure?" he asked.

"Always."

"I think I'm in love with you," he said.

She stilled. The color and smile drained from her face. He wasn't even sure if she was breathing.

His heart shot like a missile to his throat. Why had he blurted it out like that?

"You don't have to say anything," he said. It was

too fast for her. She needed baby steps. But also, the truth. "I get what I said might be scary for you. You're gun-shy about relationships, even though you're not timid about anything else in your life. This is new for me, too." He hadn't gotten serious about anyone. Until now. "My heart is every bit as much in your hands as yours is in mine. Okay?"

"How can you be sure it's love? It's only been a few days."

When you know, you know.

"It's actually been almost a year. I fell for you the first time I saw you sparring in USD. Then at the gala, well, I fell much, much harder." A complete goner. "I've never felt like this. I wanted you to know." He just hoped she didn't run.

She moistened her lips. "No heavy discussions allowed before breakfast. New rule."

Rules were a good sign. He could live with that.

"How about you pick up some food from Delgado's?" she suggested. "We could eat together at USD."

Even better, she wasn't running. He smiled. "I like your idea." He kissed her again.

She snatched the cowboy hat from his head and put it on. "I'll hang on to this for you."

"My hat looks good on you."

Her mouth curved into a slight smile.

Brian watched her get in the Jeep and drive off. He followed her. They were going in the same direction. Delgado's was just down the block from USD.

Since she hadn't told him what she wanted to eat,

he got two different things. A breakfast burrito and prairie rose special: two eggs any style, hash browns and bacon. He'd eat whichever one she didn't want.

At USD, she took the burrito, but he suspected it was because it left one of her hands free to log into her computer.

"I noticed the note on the door about closing early the next few nights."

Taking another bite, she nodded. "Until I find out what happened to Haley. Or Seth's arrested."

"Both could take a while."

"That's not what I want to hear."

"I know." He finished eating and wiped his mouth with a napkin. "Have you ever considered taking a full day off, on a regular basis?"

"Why? Did you have plans for me?"

"A few dirty thoughts spring to mind," he said, and she grinned. "But I'm talking about time to recharge. Unwind. I'd love to spend a full day with you."

"Sounds nice. Let me think on it."

The front door opened. One of her trainers walked in, and she waved to him.

"I need to tell Dustin about Teddy." She stood and came around the desk. "I can't believe I was this close to firing Teddy in a voice mail for not showing up." Taking the hat off, she set it on his head.

Brian watched her approach Dustin and put a hand on his shoulder as she spoke to him.

A phone buzzed.

He checked his pocket, but it wasn't his. Looking around, he spotted Charlie's on the desk, but it wasn't that one either.

The buzzing came from inside her duffel bag on the desk. He unzipped it and took out the burner.

"Charlie!" He held up the phone, and she nodded.

She said something else to Dustin, who had lowered his head, his face in shock. She hurried into the office and grabbed the phone.

"Hey, Orson. Did you find something?" She listened. Then her gaze flashed up to Brian's. She nodded, grabbed a pen and wrote on a notepad. "You're the best." She smirked like Orson had responded with something saucy. "Knock it off. I've got to go. Thank you." She clicked off, flipped the phone closed and shoved it back in her bag. "Haley is alive. And Orson found her."

A wunderkind indeed.

"PULL OVER THERE and park," Charlie said to Brian, gesturing to the diner situated next to a gas station.

"Why?" he asked. "The motel is across the street."

"Please, just do it."

His jaw hardened, but he did as she asked. "Are you going to tell me why we're parked at this diner?"

"If Haley sees a cop before I've had a chance to talk to her and convince her that she can trust you, it's possible she might not tell me anything. But it's certain that she'll freak out." Charlie had plenty of questions, and she intended to get answers. "Give me twenty minutes with her. Then we'll either come to you or I'll call you and have you pull the car around. Okay?"

By the look on his face, she could tell that he didn't like it. "No. Not okay. I'm parking at the motel." He put the vehicle in reverse and backed away from the diner. "I'll position the truck where she won't be able to see me from the room. *Okay?*"

Not that he was truly asking because he was already pulling into the lot.

"What's the room number?" he asked.

She glanced down at the piece of paper in her hand that had the address of the motel in Kimball, Nebraska, less than two hours from Laramie. Brian had been right to expand the search radius, and she was grateful that Orson had come through, finding her.

The motel was right off the highway, not far after entering Nebraska from Wyoming.

"One twenty-five."

He parked in front of room 103 near the front office. "Haley's room should be all the way at the other end."

"Why couldn't you park across the street like I wanted?" she asked.

Unclicking his seat belt, he shifted to look at her and propped his forearm on the back of the seat. "Because I've got an uneasy feeling in my gut. Combine that with your penchant for finding trouble, and being across the street felt too far. Call it being caution, protective, whatever you want. But if you insist

on going in there alone, this is how it's going to be."
He tipped his hat at her.

She groaned, torn between arguing with him and
kissing him. "Twenty minutes."

"You've got ten. Then we're bringing her in to
DCI Powell."

Sighing, she slid out of the truck.

"Hey, be careful," he said. "When you first knock,
don't stand directly in front of the door."

"Why not?"

"You don't know what's on the other side. She
could be armed and jumpy. Not a good combination."

Charlie nodded, closed the door and hurried down
the walkway. The High Point motel looked as if it had
seen better days. Old and run-down it had plenty of
vacancies, judging by the nearly empty lot.

Drawing closer to the end of the building, she
eyed the truck in front of the last door. A Ford F-150.
Dark green. Older model. She knew the plate number.

Teddy's truck. Was he alive, too, and hiding out
with Haley?

Rushing up to room 125, she noticed that the sheer
curtains were drawn across the window, but not the
heavy blackout drapes. A television was on inside.

She knocked, standing off to the side near the
window while she did it. "Haley!"

No answer.

"Haley!" She knocked again. "It's me, Charlie.
Open up."

She strained to listen. No movement on the other

side of the door. The only sound she picked up was the whoosh of the traffic on Old Highway 71. Charlie turned and stared at the Ford behind her.

"Haley, it's just me, Charlie." She pounded her fist. "Are you in there?"

The sound of the television died. Rustling inside the room. Maybe one person.

"Open this door!"

A chain slid back and rattled. The door swung open, and there stood Haley, pointing a Smith & Wesson .357 level at her chest. "What are you doing here?"

"I could ask you the same question. Unless you're going to shoot me, lower that thing."

"Are you here alone?"

Charlie swallowed. She didn't want to lie, but she also didn't want to spook Haley by telling her that her companion was a detective who worked with her husband. "Do you see me with anyone?"

Wide-eyed and hair mussed, Haley stuck her head out the door and took a furtive glance around.

"Satisfied?" Charlie strode past her into the room.

Haley slammed the door, locked it and slipped the chain on with a shaky hand. "How did you find me?"

"That doesn't matter right now. What matters is that I did."

Trembling, Haley plopped down on the bed, clutching the revolver. She didn't look well. Pale skin. Bags under her eyes. She was bare foot and wore a T-shirt and jeans.

Charlie looked around.

The dim motel room smelled of mildew and traces of a hundred seedy encounters. Empty bags of junk food and cans of diet cola were on the nightstand.

"Tell me what you did." Charlie crossed her arms. "And why you did it."

Haley bent over, propped her elbow on her thigh and dropped her head into her palm.

"You better start talking," Charlie demanded. "What happened after you called Wednesday night?"

"I staged the scene at the house."

"You baited me and set me up."

Raising her head, a stranger with a steely glint in her eyes stared back. "Yeah, I baited you. But I was setting up Seth. Not you."

"Why?"

"Because he deserves it!" Haley jumped to her feet. "He's a soulless beast. He killed Teddy!"

It was true? "How do you know for sure?" Charlie didn't want it to be real. She wanted to cling to hope that he was still alive.

"Seth bragged about it. Taunted me with the fact that he killed him. After that I realized it didn't matter if my name changed, if I looked different, if I lived somewhere else. He would always find me."

"But we had a plan. It would've kept you safe."

"To hell with your plan."

All the effort and time and money that had gone into the process—wasted. The months of manipulation that Haley had invested in getting Charlie to even help her in the first place. For what? "Why come to me to begin with?" Then a sneaking suspicion settled in her gut like a rock. "How did you even know to come to me, that I could help you disappear?"

"My friend Rafe. You helped his cousin. Eva Johnson."

Eva's maiden name had been Martinez. But it was a common surname. Charlie hadn't made the connection. "Well then, you know how my system works. Why didn't you believe in it?"

"I did. I thought it could work, too. Then Seth took Teddy away from me." Haley seemed to collapse in on herself. "Seth can take anything away. Even my life." Tears glistened in her eyes and rolled down her cheeks. "I needed him to pay. Finally. For something. I don't know what he did with Teddy's body. Whether there's evidence of his murder somewhere.

"Speaking of evidence, do you have any on Seth that could put him away?"

Haley lowered her head. "Yeah, but…" She chewed her bottom lip. "Other people I know working for him will be hurt by it. They'll go to jail, too."

"People like Aubrey?"

Haley's shocked gaze flashed up to her. She nodded. "That's why I needed him to be convicted and jailed for something else. Like my *murder*. He deserves to rot in prison for all his crimes."

Charlie paced in the room, fuming at the lies and deception. "There was so much blood at the house. How did you pull that off?"

Grabbing a tissue, Haley sniffled. "I volunteer at the hospital. I got to know people. There was a phlebotomist with a gambling debt. I paid him to draw as much blood as possible from me. Two pints. But it wasn't enough. I bought two more pints of someone else's blood. That's why I needed the house to explode. To make sure the police couldn't analyze all of it. Only mine, which I mostly used on the porch and in the grass. A bit in the kitchen."

Every word out of Haley's conniving mouth infuriated Charlie. "Why rope me into this? Was the abuse even real?"

"Yes," Haley said, shaking the gun. "Seth not only beat me, but he got into my head. Never let me forget how small and insignificant I am. That the only value I have is what he gives me." More tears.

"Why me?" Charlie scrubbed the heel of her palm across her forehead. "You have family that you could've dragged into this. Called them to come running out to your house that night."

Haley shook her head. "Seth doesn't let them visit. They never would've come. But I knew you would. Knew that you wouldn't call the cops."

A sickening thought occurred to Charlie as the pieces came together. "Did you shoot at me, too, at my house?"

Haley sobbed now. "I'm sorry. I'm so ashamed."

"But why?" A misdirected bullet could've killed her. Or Brian. How could Haley have taken such a crazy chance?

"It made you angry, didn't it?" Haley dabbed at the tears and wiped her nose. "Fired you up with the determination to get Seth?"

And it had.

This woman was a master manipulator.

What was the point of asking her any questions? It would only be more manipulation. Spinning half-truths just like Aubrey.

"You're a real piece of work, lady." Charlie was disgusted with herself for being so stupid. So easy. "There's a DCI agent, Logan Powell, looking for you."

"What?" Haley asked, a horrified look coming over her face.

"He doesn't think you're dead. Convinced me to look for you."

"Wait a minute," Haley said, her tears drying up quicker than a mirage in the desert. "If DCI Powell thought you could find me, who else might think the same? Did you lead someone here? Seth? One of his people? Oh God, the cartel?" Haley spun around. "The money."

"What money?"

BRIAN KEPT CHECKING his mirrors. But the itchy sensation slithering up and down his spine didn't stop.

He climbed out of his truck and stretched his legs. Glancing over at the front office, he spotted the coffee machine. He checked his watch. Charlie had two more minutes with Haley, and then he was knocking on the door.

Time enough for a cup of Joe. He stepped inside and went over to the small table set up for guests. As he poured coffee in a paper cup, he looked across the street.

Was that the same black SUV sitting at the gas station that had pulled in around the same time he parked at the diner?

He couldn't be sure. It was a Chevy. Dark tinted windows. They were a dime a dozen. He hadn't gotten the license plate. But it was in the exact same spot off to the side of the pumps.

They hadn't been followed from the house. That he was certain of. But it was entirely possible someone might have been waiting near USD. It was common knowledge that she went there every day. The best place to find her if someone was looking.

On the freeway he hadn't noticed a tail.

Sipping his coffee, he watched the SUV pull out of the parking spot and leave the gas station. Relief ebbed through him.

Until the vehicle crossed over Old Highway 71 and careened into the motel lot. The driver gunned the gas, tires screeching across the asphalt.

Brian sprinted to the door and bounded out into the lot.

A window in the back driver's side of the vehicle rolled down, and the barrel of an automatic weapon stuck out.

Terror clawed at Brian's chest as he dropped the cup.

A series of loud *RAT-A-TAT-TATS* exploded.

Bullets tore into room 125, riddling the door with holes and busting the window.

No! Charlie!

He drew his weapon and returned fire, shattering the rear windshield.

The vehicle took off, speeding out of the lot. As it turned, going around the corner, he caught a glimpse of a man. The one with a jagged scar on his face.

Brian bolted across the lot. He kicked in what was left of the door to room 125. His gaze flew around. Bullet holes everywhere. Shattered lamps. Busted TV. Feathers floated in the air.

"Charlie!" he screamed, racing around the bed. Charlie and Haley were on the floor.

Blood was splattered on both of them.

Chapter Thirteen

In the Kimball emergency waiting room, Brian threw his arms around Charlie, thankful that she wasn't hurt.

"I'm okay," she said, again, for like the twentieth time.

But he didn't believe it until an EMT had checked her.

The blood on her body had been Haley's. Other than a gash on her forehead from hitting her head on the nightstand as she fell, and a few stitches to close it, she was fine.

He stared at the stitches and caressed her cheek.

She looked composed, but he saw the nerves beneath the surface. "If not for Haley—" she paused, swallowed "—shoving me to the ground, I might be in surgery with her." She looked up at him, and the misery in her eyes made his chest squeeze. "I led them straight to her."

"We led them."

DCI Powell, who had arrived after Brian called him, spun on his heel. "This wouldn't have happened if you had notified me of her whereabouts as soon as you had located her. We would've brought her in quietly. Safely."

That was probably true. But Charlie had legitimate concerns about the way Haley had been handled by Logan Powell's task force. Charlie felt better about bringing her in herself, and Brian had agreed to help her.

Haley had lost a lot of blood, for real this time, in the motel room and on the way to the hospital. Now she might not pull through the surgery.

He still couldn't swallow the story Charlie had repeated about all the things that Haley had done. The way she had taken advantage of Charlie's need to help victims of domestic abuse burned him to the bone.

The entrance doors to the ER whooshed open.

Kent strode inside. "I got here as fast as I could."

"You called Detective Kramer?" Powell asked.

"I did. He's my partner on the Haley Olsen case. You don't suspect that he's dirty, do you?"

The DCI agent clenched his jaw. "He's not under investigation or suspicion."

"Then I trust there isn't a problem here."

"Make no mistake, there is a problem. With the way you violated protocol, by taking your girlfriend on a road trip to see my informant, when you should have contacted me."

"This is my fault," Charlie said to Powell. "Not Brian's. I didn't trust you to have Haley's best interest at heart."

Brian wasn't going to allow her to blame herself for this.

He stared at Powell, forcing himself to keep his cool. "She's the one who found her. Something you couldn't do. Your mistake, or someone on your task force, is the reason Haley bolted. I'm certain that leaking to her husband that she was having an affair is violation of protocol. It's also what got Teddy Williams killed. So, if we're making a tally of mistakes here, I'd say that you and your task force have a longer column."

"For the record, the agent who leaked the information has been suspended pending an investigation."

As Brian had suspected. "You lied."

"I did what I had to get your girlfriend to cooperate." He stepped away.

"Is Charlie all right?" Kent asked, easing forward.

Brian nodded. He looked at her again, hating how close she had come to dying. How helpless he had felt. The desperation that had flooded him at the prospect of losing her. He brushed his knuckles across her bloodstained cheek before going over to the other detective.

"I can't believe you two found Haley Olsen and left me out of the road trip."

Maybe he should've brought Kent along. Another set of eyes keeping watch might have prevented this.

A doctor wearing scrubs pushed through doors and approached them. "You're waiting for information on Haley Olsen?"

They all nodded. Charlie rose and came to Brian's side.

"A bullet ruptured her subclavian artery," the doctor said. "She lost a tremendous amount of blood. Almost didn't make it. But the surgery went well. We were able to repair the damage and stop the bleeding. Then we gave her a transfusion of two units. She should fully recover."

Charlie leaned against Brian as if a burden had been lifted off her shoulders.

"When can I speak with her?" DCI Powell said. "I have some urgent questions."

"She's in the recovery room now. She'll be a bit groggy for a while."

"That's fine. I might get more truthful responses if she's kind of out of it," Powell said. "Also, when will she be able to leave the hospital?"

"Not for a couple of days."

"We'd prefer to have her in a safe house, but we'll need to make arrangements to have her airlifted out of here as soon as possible to another hospital for her safety."

"Oh," the doctor said. "I didn't realize. It is possible to have her recover at a safe house, provided you have a nurse available for a couple of days who could change her IV and the dressing for her wound."

Powell nodded. "I can make that happen."

"Come with me. I'll take you to see her."

"Wait," Charlie said, going up to Powell. "She mentioned that she had evidence on Seth, but that she was worried about implicating people she cared about."

"My people are going through the motel room with a fine-tooth comb. The one thing your boyfriend did right was ensuring the police kept officers posted at the room. If she had any evidence in there, we'll find it. And if it's somewhere else, I will persuade her that it's in her best interest to cooperate and hand it over."

"Also, one of the last things she said to me was something about the cartel and money."

"Do you know what she meant?" Powell asked.

"She didn't get a chance to explain because gunfire turned the room into Swiss cheese and nearly us along with it."

"I'm glad you two are okay." Powell clutched her arm. "Thank you for finding her." He left with the doctor.

Brian put an arm around Charlie, bringing her close. "Please tell me that you intend to take the rest of the day off. We'll go back to my place. Decompress."

She shook her head. "We've got booked classes this afternoon through the early evening, and Dustin has to leave by four. Decompressing will have to wait."

"At least let me take you to get cleaned up first." He looked over her bloodstained clothes. "Shower and change."

"Yeah, that's what I had in mind."

"To reiterate what the DCI agent said, I'm glad

you two are all right also." Kent glanced between them. "Didn't know you were dating anyone," he said to Brian. "But good to see that you're putting yourself out there."

Not sure what to say, Brian simply nodded.

"I never showed you all the pictures I took of Seth," Charlie said. "And the people he's been associating with. Especially at those suspicious addresses."

"We'll take a look at when we get to the house," Brian said. He turned to Kent. "If there's anything worthwhile, I'll share it with you."

"Sounds good. In the meantime, we've got reports to fill out," Kent said. "I'll get started since you'll be *delayed*."

"Sure. The only thing is we need to keep all this from spreading around in the department. Especially the part about the DCI investigating Seth Olsen."

"I won't submit it through regular channels. Only the lieutenant and chief of police will see it."

"Works for me," Brian said.

AFTER COMING SO close to death, Charlie was astounded by the numbness that kept threatening to engulf her. Every time she felt the cold sinking in, right down to her core, she thought about Brian. His warmth. His light.

And it helped to plug her back in.

Is that what she had been doing since her mother's murder? Disconnecting?

Such a sad way to live.

She glanced at the USD schedule on her computer.

No one was on the books for the last two classes this evening. This was the one night a week where Rocco would usually take over as the instructor and close up for her if he was available. She hadn't realized how much she missed those evening hours off until now.

Changes needed to be made in her schedule so she could actually have time for a life. The school didn't need to be open seven days a week. Maybe she'd shut down on Mondays. Hire a dedicated trainer to teach three to four evenings as well as handle locking up the school.

She wanted time. To slow down and unwind. To spend with Brian, hanging out on his back porch, curled up in his arms.

Who would have ever thought she'd feel that way about anyone, much less a cop?

Charlie thought about the pictures she'd shown Brian. He'd been able to identify two other detectives, who were also possibly dirty. When he'd pointed to the one with close-cropped dark blond hair, Colvin, she'd caught a flash of anger in his eyes. She hadn't understood until he explained that Colvin was Seth's alibi. The balding guy with a paunch was a detective, too. Eklund.

But Brian hadn't recognized the man with glasses.

Haley needed to come through and nail all these guys.

Charlie went to the first of two private training rooms for one-on-one sessions and started putting away equipment: pads, mats, sparring helmets.

"Hello," a female voice called out.

Charlie shut off the light in the room and stepped out into the main area where they held group classes.

"Hi." It was Aubrey. "Do you have a minute?" she asked.

This was the first time Charlie had seen her in regular clothes, a formfitting dress and heels. But it was even more surprising to see her standing in USD.

"Sure," Charlie said.

"I'm sorry I lied to you about Haley and about spying on Seth. It's just that my position is delicate. You came around asking dangerous questions, where I work. The last person I gave information to disappeared."

In hindsight, Charlie would've handled things differently. "I understand. I shouldn't have popped back up at the club the way that I did."

"No, you shouldn't have," Aubrey said, with a frown. "But I get why you did. We're both worried about Haley. She's lucky to have someone like you on her side. Have you found out anything more? Do you know if Haley is dead or alive?"

A chill moved through Charlie like someone had walked over her grave. She tensed. Hesitated. "She's alive. But I can't say anything more than that. To protect her."

Aubrey exhaled a big breath, relief washing over her face. "Thank goodness she's all right. If anything had happened to her, I don't know what I would do."

"You don't need to worry about her. She's going

to be okay." Charlie waited to see if this supposed friend kept pushing for information or let it be.

"Do you think I could start taking some classes here? It'd be nice to learn how to defend myself."

"Of course," Charlie said, feeling more relaxed at the change in conversation. "Everyone is welcome. Your first two will be free."

"That's real nice of you." Aubrey smiled. "Mind if I use the bathroom before I leave?"

"Go right ahead. The restroom is around the corner and down the hall."

Aubrey's heels clacked away against the linoleum, and Charlie went to the second training room. Once she was done packing up the equipment, she grabbed the laundry bag.

"Good night," Aubrey called out.

"Night!"

As Charlie stuffed dirty towels in the bag that she'd drop off at the cleaners in the morning, she thought she heard the door again.

"Aubrey?" Charlie switched off the light in the room and headed back into the main area.

No sign of her. There was no one outside on the sidewalk. The space inside was still. Yet, something tickled at her senses.

Her cell phone rang. She hurried to her office and dumped the laundry bag in front of her desk. Seeing Brian's name on the caller ID made her smile. "Hey. I'm locking up now."

"How does homemade wood-fired pizza sound for dinner?" Brian asked.

"Delicious." Right on cue, her stomach grumbled. "I'm starving."

"Excellent," he said. "I just finished making the dough. What's your preference for toppings?"

"I'm easy. Anything except pineapple."

"My kind of woman." His whiskey and velvet voice sent a tingle through her.

Her smile deepened.

"Just to give you a heads-up," he said, "I think we should talk after dinner." His tone was easy-breezy.

She loved the way he kept things light. "Is that a euphemism or is this going to be an actual conversation?" she asked.

"A conversation. About things. About us. But we could make it pillow talk."

That was the best kind. "The forewarning is appreciated." But unnecessary. When it came to Brian, she wanted to run to him. Not away from him. Not anymore. "See you soon." She disconnected.

She grabbed her duffel bag, left the office and locked the front door.

Switching off the interior lights, she peered into the darkness out front, listening, looking. Nothing appeared amiss.

Curiosity poked at her. She opened the GPS app on her phone and stared at the map. Seth's truck was out at the ranch. Actually, his brother's piece of land. The first time she'd seen it there since she'd been surveilling him.

Still, something wasn't right. She unzipped her

duffel bag, dropping her cell phone inside and pulling out her .45.

Heading for the back door, she passed the bathroom. She reached for the dead bolt on the back door and froze.

It was already unlocked. Her gaze flew to the alarm keypad on the wall. The screen was blank. No green light. The security system had been disabled.

The hair on the nape of her neck rose.

Clutching the SIG in both hands now, she crept backward from the door. Not knowing what, or rather who, was waiting to ambush her on the other side in the dark parking lot.

The door swung open. She sucked in a breath.

Two men wearing black ski masks stood across the threshold.

She took aim. A creak came from behind her. Dread spilled down her spine. She turned.

A third man lunged from the bathroom, tackling her.

The gun went off. They crashed to the floor. Air whooshed from her lungs as he landed on her with sickening force. Pain sliced through her.

They wrestled over the gun. She threw an elbow to her attacker's face, but he slammed her forearm against the floor. Her .45 went skittering.

A different man grabbed her ankles, trying to pin her down. She lashed out with a foot. Her heel hit flesh. The man groaned. Another knelt beside her. The dark figure loomed over Charlie, holding something in his hands.

She kicked and punched, battling to twist free. Desperate to escape their grasp, but it was three against one. *Cowards.*

Duct tape was pressed to her mouth and a black hood was shoved over her head. Three sets of hands tossed her onto her stomach. A knee was thrust into her spine. The man's weight bore down on her, flattening her against the floor, until there was no more air. She couldn't breathe. Couldn't scream.

Zip ties tightened around her wrists, pinching down to the bone. They restrained her ankles next and hoisted her up.

She struggled to move her arms, her legs. To keep fighting.

It was futile, but she refused to stop.

Something hit the side of her head. The darkness lurched. She tried to hang on to the threads of consciousness unraveling, but failed.

WHERE WAS SHE?

His tenth time calling Charlie, and she still didn't answer the phone. Brian hung up again. After the pizza had grown cold and he hadn't been able to reach her, he'd gotten into his truck.

He zipped down Third Street and turned into the parking lot behind USD, tires screeching. Slamming on the brake, he stopped next to Dustin's SUV.

The back door was wide open.

Drawing his firearm, Brian hopped out of his truck.

"Charlie!" he shouted as he ran inside the building. "Are you here?"

Nothing.

"Charlie!" He swept the corridor with his gaze. Fumbled for a light switch. Found it.

Brian's blood ran cold as he took in the scene.

Everything stood out in jarring relief. Her duffel bag was on the floor. Unzipped. The .45 SIG Sauer she carried was against a baseboard. Black scuff marks on the linoleum. A bullet hole in the drywall.

Fear tightened in his gut as he peered in the bag. Inside were clothes, her wallet and cell phone.

She wouldn't go anywhere without it. She certainly wouldn't leave a loaded weapon on the floor.

Oh, God. Charlie.

Seth must've taken her.

A hard lump rose in his throat. His mind whirled, the detective part of his brain strategizing how to possibly find her.

She didn't have her phone. Wherever he took her would be out of town, beyond traffic cameras. Limiting Brian's ability to track her.

He growled his frustration. *Think, think.* Drawing in a deep breath, he clenched his fist tighter.

An idea came to him. A long shot. But possible.

He knelt by her bag, rummaged through it until he found her burner phone and dialed the one person who might be able to help him save the woman he loved.

"Hey, beautiful," Orson said. "Did everything work out with your girl?"

"My name is Brian Bradshaw. You don't know me, but—"

"Then we shouldn't be talking," the man said. "Especially not from this number."

"Orson, don't hang up. Charlie is in danger. She needs your help. It's life or death."

Silence.

It was better than a dial tone.

Brian pulled out his cell and fired off a text message to Kent.

"What do you need from me?" Orson finally asked.

"For you to do what you do best. Hack her cell phone. Her laptop. Something."

"What you're asking is illegal. Are you a cop?"

Brian cursed as something in his chest wilted. "This isn't entrapment."

"I take that as a *yes* and it would make this a classic example of entrapment."

Damn it. "You're right. Entrapment is illegal. Therefore, you've got a solid defense for any potential criminal charges. But if you don't help me, Charlie is going to die. And I'm willing to risk prison to keep that from happening."

More silence. But Orson didn't hang up.

"Please," Brian said. "I'm begging you."

"What are you looking for on her phone and laptop?" Orson asked.

"Someone's kidnapped her. He's going to hurt her. Then kill her. I need to find her before that happens. But the only thing on her person that I can think of to locate her is her smartwatch. The app linked to it will be on her phone and laptop. I need you to access the app. It'll show her GPS location. Can you?"

"Yeah, I think so."

Think wasn't good enough. "This needs to happen. Now," Brian snapped. "The sooner the better. Understand?"

"The thing is, you need to find her ASAP and that'll take too long."

If Seth had Charlie, this might be their only chance of getting her back. It might already be too late, but Brian wasn't going to give up. He wanted to yell, to punch the wall, to find Seth and put an end to this, but he took a deep breath. Strained for self-control. "I need you to find her. There has to be some way. Charlie said you're a prodigy. Some kind of genius." Even after their breakup, Charlie still worked with him, believed in his skills.

"There is a way," Orson said. "Faster, too. We don't need to go through her cell or the laptop. What kind of smartwatch is she wearing?"

Brian told him the brand.

Rapid-fire clicking on a keyboard sounded over the phone. "She hasn't changed," Orson said. "I'm pulling up the website now. She uses the same email as her log-in for stuff like this. All I have to do is crack her password for this site. And bingo. Pull up her location."

"Then do it. Hurry. *Please.*"

"I have to ask, who is Charlie to you?"

Everything. His heart squeezed at the realization. "She's my future."

"Well, that explains the stern talk she had with me. Put me in my place. It was overdue. Are you going to make an honest woman out of her?"

He caught the double entendre. One day, he'd love to make Charlie his wife and have her operate above-board. No more gray boxes. "Yes."

But first they had to reach her in time.

Chapter Fourteen

Charlie's head throbbed. She swallowed. Her tongue felt heavy, her throat dry as cotton as she came to in confusion. *In darkness.*

What was happening?

Men in ski masks.

At USD.

It came back to her in a rush.

She tried to sit up, but she was on her belly, with legs bound and arms restrained behind her back. Duct tape over her mouth. In a vehicle.

She could tell from the sounds, the movement. The change in inertia pitched her to the side, jostling her body.

"I don't understand why you need me." A woman's voice. *Aubrey.* "I did my part like you told me. Just let me go. Please."

Aubrey had helped them get in. The conversation, talking about wanting to take classes, asking to the use the bathroom, had all been a ruse. To give her a chance to unlock the back door for those men.

And Charlie had fallen for it. How stupid could she be.

"There's something else I need you to do first," a man said.

At the sound of that voice, Charlie's heart dropped. *Seth Olsen.*

His truck was at his brother's ranch, but he hadn't been there. Instead, he'd been lurking behind USD, waiting to ambush her. Had he found the GPS tracker?

"What else?" Aubrey asked, her voice panicked. "Tell me and I'll do it, so I can get out of here."

"You'll find out soon enough," Seth said. "We're almost there. In the meantime, be a good girl and keep your mouth shut."

Momentum rolled Charlie to the side. They were turning. From the change in the sound of the tires, they had left a paved road for a dirt one. A little bumpy, too, as they continued along it for a while.

Finally, the vehicle came to a stop.

"Get her up and out," Seth ordered.

There was a tug at her ankles, and the restraint fell away. Someone had cut the zip tie, but her wrists were still bound together.

The hood was snatched from her head. She blinked, getting her bearings. Her gaze flew around wildly. She was on the floor of a cargo van.

A man wrenched open the side door and grabbed her arm. "Come on." He hauled her out of the van.

Cool night air brushed her face. A stark relief from the hot hood that had been suffocating. In the bright moonlight, her vision cleared. They were in the woods.

None of the men wore their masks. She was able to make them out clearly.

Seth led the way down a path. Detective Colvin shoved Aubrey forward, causing her to stumble in her heels while Detective Eklund kept a tight grip on Charlie as he hurried her along.

The fact that they were no longer hiding their identities meant they didn't intend for her to survive this encounter. Charlie swallowed the bile in her throat.

She wasn't ready to die. Not like this.

Brian. The thought of never seeing him again was too much to bear.

The meaty hand on her arm jerked her forward. They passed Seth's truck along with two other vehicles.

The air held an unpleasant stench that only became fouler the closer they got to a barn. A cacophony of squeals and grunts rose, filling the air. As they came around the side of the barn, about two dozen pink hogs came into view.

The pigpen was dimly lit by the flames crackling in a stone firepit.

Charlie tugged her arms, trying to weaken the zip tie. Maybe she could pop it if she got her wrists at the right angle and put enough force behind it, or wriggle one hand out. She dug her heels in the dirt and tilted back to slow down their approach.

Eklund yanked her to his side, nearly taking her off her feet.

"Do we need to worry about your brother coming out here?" Colvin asked.

"No," Seth said. "I keep Abel out of this. He doesn't know anything. Only to stay inside the house when I'm out here working."

Colvin released Aubrey, and she stopped near the firepit.

"Now what?" Aubrey asked.

"We wait for the rest of our party to join us," Seth said, glancing at his watch. "Should be here any minute. He's always punctual."

Charlie glanced around. Forced herself to concentrate. Sharpen her senses. She needed to think of a way out of this. Find an advantage.

The farmhouse was about two hundred feet upwind from the pigpen. Seth's brother lived there. If she got free somehow and made it to the house, she could call for help if there was a landline. But would she be able to make it with three armed men in pursuit?

A vehicle approached. Headlights cut through the darkness, drawing closer. The SUV stopped. The engine cut off. A car door slammed shut.

Someone heavy-footed came up the path. A man wearing a white button-down and slacks came into the light of the fire. Blond and balding. Average height. Lanky.

Charlie recognized him from the photos. He was the unidentified man.

"What in the hell is going on?" he asked, his gaze

bouncing between Aubrey and Charlie. "What are they doing here?"

"We've got some business to take care of," Seth said.

"I don't get involved with this side of things." The guy backed up, raising his palms. "Just give me my cut. That's why I'm here. Then I'm gone."

"This does involve you. She's been taking pictures!" Seth pointed to Charlie. "Of us together. Including you."

His gaze swept to Charlie, his eyes growing wide with panic. "What?" He turned to Seth. "I can't be implicated in any of this. I'll be disbarred. I could go to jail. You have to handle it."

This was their lawyer. The one who was helping them make all this possible. There must have been layers of legal red tape used to hide their identities with the offshore shell companies.

"That's what I'm doing. Fixing it." Seth put a hand on the wood rail of the pigpen and leaned against it. "Come here," he said to Aubrey, beckoning to her with a gloved hand.

"Please. Let me go," she said. "I told you a million times that I'm sorry."

"Don't make me tell you twice."

Trembling, Aubrey treaded carefully over to him, holding out one arm to maintain her balance on the uneven ground and clutching her purse with the other.

"Good girl," Seth said, like she was dog, and Charlie gritted her teeth. "Give me that switchblade you carry around all the time."

Tears leaked from Aubrey's eyes. "Remember I was the one who told you to watch out for her. That she was following you. Taking pictures of you. Of all of you," she said, pointing a finger at Colvin and Eklund.

"Only after she made that little scene inside the club," Seth said. "When you had no other choice but to tell me."

"I never should have talked to her." Aubrey glared at Charlie, and then looked back at Seth. "Lesson learned," she sobbed. "Okay."

Seth held out his palm. "I'm waiting."

With shaking hands, Aubrey unzipped her purse and gave him the knife. "You've got to believe me," she pleaded. "It'll never happen again."

"I know it won't." Seth smiled as he caressed her cheek. In the firelight, his eyes were dark and empty like those of a snake. "Because I'm going to make sure of it." He pressed the button on the handle. The blade slashed out with a *flick*.

"What are you doing?" the lawyer asked, a terrified look stretching across his face.

Aubrey cringed. "But why?" she cried. "I didn't tell her anything useful."

"No loose ends." Seth slit her jugular in one smooth motion.

Gurgling blood, Aubrey clutched her throat.

Charlie reeled back in horror, but Eklund's tight hold on her didn't let her take more than two steps.

"What the…" The lawyer stumbled away from the firepit.

Seth shoved Aubrey backward, over the top rail into the pen.

The pigs surged, swarming all over the body, in a snarling, squealing frenzy.

Disgust and rage rolled through Charlie.

"Have you lost your mind?" the lawyer screamed. "You murdered her. This is crazy!"

"Shut up, Alcock." Seth pointed the switchblade at him. "I'm working. Trying to clean up this mess."

"I didn't sign on for this!" Alcock started hyperventilating. "You've made me an accessory!"

"Now your hands are just as dirty as ours," Eklund said, sneering. "Covered in blood."

Alcock swore. "You dragged me here to set me up?"

"Be quiet," Seth ordered.

The men stopped arguing. The sound of jostling, grunting and squeals drew everyone's attention to the swine in the pen.

"Did you know pigs are opportunistic omnivores?" Seth asked, now stalking toward her. "They'll eat almost anything they can chew. Even bone."

Charlie's stomach heaved. She thought she might puke.

Stepping in front of her, he obscured the light of the fire. He was a big guy. Broad-shouldered and muscular. A dark nightmare. "I have my brother keep them a little hungry. For times such as these, when I need them for disposal. Even with twenty-six of them, it'll take hours for them to finish. They haven't eaten this good since I fed them Teddy."

Oh, God. Teddy really was dead. Not missing. Haley had been telling the truth.

Alcock put a hand over his mouth like he was going to be sick.

Still holding the bloody knife, Seth gripped her chin, and she flinched. "There's no way out of this for you Charlotte."

Hearing her full name that no one ever used sent a fresh jolt of fear through her.

"You're as good as dead," Seth said, and a knot swelled in her chest, tightening through her rib cage. "But *how* you go is up to you. I can strip you naked. Cut your Achilles tendons and toss you in the pen with your hands bound. That'll be agonizingly slow. Excruciating. But fun to watch."

Her skin turned to ice.

"I wouldn't wish that on anybody. Or…" He paused as a smile stretched across his ugly mouth. "It can be quick and painless." Releasing her chin, he put the knife away. He pulled a pack of cigarettes from his cargo pants. Tapped one out. Lit the cigarette from the fire in the stone pit. All while the pigs did their ghoulish work, the sound of crunching bone piercing the night. "Your choice," he said, his tone taunting as he prowled back over.

Pulse pounding at her temples, her head aching, she wished her hands were free and this was a one-on-one fight.

Seth sucked in a deep drag on his cigarette. Held

her gaze. Exhaled through his mouth, blowing a cloud of smoke in her face.

She'd held her breath but coughed, nonetheless.

"All you have to do is tell me where I can find Haley," he said, like a used-car salesman trying to make a deal that only benefited himself.

Seth reached for her and ripped the duct tape from her lips.

Fire bloomed across her mouth. She sucked in a breath. Gasped from the lingering smoke in the air.

He bent closer, reeking of gin and sweat that almost made her gag as her stomach clenched. "So, what do you say?"

Nerves shooting into overdrive, Charlie said, "Drop dead."

No matter what she told him, he was going to kill her anyway.

"Bad choice." Seth punched her in the stomach.

Pain tore through her abdomen, stealing her breath, blurring her vision as she dropped to her knees. He snatched her by her hair and yanked her back up to her feet.

"I never did care for a woman with too much fire in her blood. Let's try again. Every time you refuse to tell me what I need to know, we'll strip an item of clothing from you. Maybe that will persuade you to talk."

DREAD BURNED IN Brian's gut as they sped down Highway 230 in his truck. What he wouldn't have given to be behind the wheel of Charlie's Hellcat instead of his vehicle. The clock ticking in his head rapped louder and louder, a bad feeling swelling in his gut.

"We'll reach her in time," Kent said from the passenger seat as though reading his mind.

They had better. For Seth's sake.

Brian believed in the law and justice. But if Seth killed Charlie, there was no power on earth that would stop Brian from getting vengeance.

He had been drawn to Charlie since he'd first seen her. Had a feeling about her. Once she had opened her mouth and snapped at him with that icy indifference, he was hooked. He hadn't been able to get her out of his head. The woman was a warrior, with steel running in her veins. But when she let her guard down, showed him how big and warm and vulnerable her heart was, he'd known…she was the one for him.

Now that she finally trusted him, finally accepted the love he had to give, he couldn't lose her. They'd barely been given a chance.

Kent had done good getting to USD within minutes of receiving Brian's text about what was happening. He looked at the smartwatch app that they'd pulled up on one of the phones. "We're only ten miles away," Kent said.

Brian didn't need the app to navigate, but they were monitoring it anyway just in case Seth moved her.

Flooring the accelerator, Brian tightened his grip on the steering wheel, his knuckles whitening. He flicked a glance in the rearview mirror. Not sure what he was expecting to see. He'd reached out to DCI Powell, who'd assured him that reinforcements would be en route to assist.

Seth Olsen wasn't operating alone. They had no idea who was with him, or how many, but it could've been half the badges in the LPD. Brian wasn't sure how far the corruption had spread. Whether it had tainted the sheriff's department. There had already been a scandal involving the previous sheriff. Brian was only willing to trust the DCI's office, but he and Kent hadn't waited for backup. There wasn't a second to spare.

"Look on the bright side. If he'd wanted to simply kill her, he could've done that at USD. Staged it like a robbery gone wrong. That would've been the cleanest way to eliminate her." Kent was continuing the pep talk he'd started after they'd raced out of the USD parking lot. "It's a good thing that he dragged her out here. Shows he's desperate. And desperation can drive a person to do dumb things. Like bringing her to his brother's ranch."

"Plenty of reasons for him to bring her out here," Brian said. "Interrogate her. Torture her. Dispose of evidence. Get rid of a body." Cold sweat slid down his spine.

"Hey, doesn't his brother have a pig farm on that ranch? I read that's how the Mob used to get rid of people in Sicily."

Brian shot him a glare. "Yeah, yeah, he does."

The car fell silent as Kent checked the app again.

Hoping that Seth wanted information out of her,

Brian pressed harder on the gas pedal, driving faster than ever before in his life. The speedometer had reached triple digits. He swerved around a sedan that was going the speed limit. At least traffic was light. One more thing, besides Orson's assistance, that was working in their favor.

"I emailed the Internal Affairs point of contact Charlie's pictures, along with the locations of the houses and businesses owned by the offshore LLC," Kent said.

It had been time that he had shared everything he'd learned with his partner.

Those pictures were the product of Charlie's snooping. Even though it had been dangerous, and he'd warned her against it, she hadn't backed down.

But that was her. Headstrong to a fault. All fire and ice. And he loved her for it.

"Good." No matter what happened tonight, the truth would come out. Every dirty cop involved was going to be exposed. "I made sure DCI Powell also got the information, too." Although he probably already had his own surveillance photos.

If not for Charlie and Haley, Seth and his crew might have gotten away with their crimes. Everything from prostitution and drugs to murder.

It sickened him that there were so many dirty cops on the force. As well as shamed him for not being more open to the idea when Charlie had suggested it. He never should've dismissed her suspicion as paranoia.

Rage replaced his gut-wrenching fear. He funneled his white-hot anger into driving.

"Any idea who the one guy in the picture is that we didn't recognize?" Kent asked.

"No, not for certain."

"We're almost there," Kent said.

Brian turned off the highway and took the road that led to the ranch. Gritting his teeth, he raced down the street. One more turn and they reached the fork where the road split for the two ranches. Killing his lights, he made a left.

He spotted an opening in the thicket on the side of the road. Pulled off into a spot in between the trees. "We should go on foot from here. Use the app to pinpoint exactly where she is on the property."

"Are you sure you don't want to wait for backup?" Kent asked.

Brian clenched his jaw. "Charlie can't afford for me to wait. But if you want to hang back until the sheriff's department arrives, I'll understand."

"We're partners on this, right." Kent his drew gun and handed him the phone with the app.

"Thanks." Brian reached into the back, snatched the one bulletproof vest that he had and offered it to his partner.

"Keep it." Kent shoved it back at him.

"We're probably outmanned and outgunned. I don't need you adding to the list of problems by taking a bullet."

"Wanna know why I drink every night?"

Brian nodded.

"To forget I have to go home to an empty house. We never had kids. Some nights I wish like hell that we had. Or at least had gotten a cat."

His grief was too fresh for Brian to point out that it wasn't too late for him to find love again. Although no one would ever replace his wife, who he'd cherished, he could still share his life with someone.

Kent gave a dry chuckle. "Put the vest on, Bradshaw. I've seen the way you look at Charlie. I remember that feeling. To have a great love is a miracle. To have it for twenty-five years was luckier than I deserved. I've got nothing to lose. You can't say the same."

Brian strapped on the vest, grabbed the extra loaded magazines, divvying them up between the two of them, and stuffed his compact backup weapon, a Beretta Nano, into his ankle holster. "When this is over, I'm buying you a cat."

Clasping his shoulder, Kent flashed a sad grin.

They both got out, closing their doors without making any noise. Brian crept through the woods, with Kent alongside him, headed toward the blinking red dot on the app.

To Charlie.

Be alive.

Please. Be alive.

No shoes, stripped down to her sports bra and underwear, Charlie shivered under Seth's hateful gaze. Rather than untie her, he'd cut her T-shirt from her with the same bloody knife that he had used to slit Aubrey's throat.

"Changed your mind? The end doesn't have to be unpleasant. But I need you tell me where my wife is hiding. She took something. I need it back."

Charlie had no idea of the location of the safe house. Even if she knew, she'd take it to the grave. Haley had made mistakes—awful, manipulative choices—but Charlie would not give her up to spare herself a nightmarish death.

"It's not as if anyone gave me the address so I could keep in touch," she said.

"Who has Haley? FBI? Marshals? Tell me the agency and name of the agent. I'll manage the rest."

She didn't want to imagine how. Bribes? Torturing others? A vicious, never-ending cycle. The buck stopped here. "You want her bad. What did she take from you? Your pride? Peace of mind?" Soon, it would be his freedom.

Seth chuckled. "She stole money. A lot of it. The cartel's cash. When they come looking for it, I need to have it."

A string of filthy curses flew from Alcock. "You didn't tell me Haley stole from the cartel. We're all as good as dead."

"Sounds like your list of problems is getting longer and longer," Charlie said to Seth. "I'll tell you what you want to know. But you've got to fight me for it. One-on-one. No restraints."

"What?" He laughed again. "You fellas believe she's actually asking me to spank her pretty butt?"

"I would've thought it would be a dream come true for you," she said. "But from the look on your face, I'd say you're scared." When he narrowed his eyes at her, jaw tightening, she knew she had him. The emotional attack worked. Such a fragile ego. Easy to bait. The hubris would do Seth in. He was so used to getting whatever he wanted, threatening, using violence, any means necessary. It's what allowed him to believe that he was above the law. That he could avoid retribution. He'd grown to see himself as invincible. "Afraid a woman will give you the beating you deserve? Should be. You pathetic excuse for a man."

Even in the dim light, she saw Seth's face redden.

"She's not going to tell you," Eklund said. "Stop toying with her. Just throw her in the pigpen and be done with it. We've wasted enough time on her."

"We need that money!" Colvin stepped toward Seth. "Or we'll be the ones in the pigpen."

"Get the lieutenant to help us," Eklund said. "He can find out who has Haley. Maybe even where they're keeping her."

Seth shook his head. "Jameson washed his hands of us the minute he learned IA was going to get involved."

"IA?" Alcock's gaze flew around, his visible panic rising.

"The lieutenant wants as much distance as possible," Seth continued. "Telling us about Haley being taken to a safe house was the last help he was willing to give." He glared at Charlie. "The agency that has her wasn't mentioned in the report. But you know, and I'm going to make you tell me."

"Make him a sweet offer he can't refuse," Eklund said, his voice desperate. "Double what he usually gets. If that doesn't work, threaten to name him as an accomplice if we all go down."

Colvin raked a hand over his close-cropped hair and paced in a circle. "Is that a joke? The lieutenant will sooner put a bullet between our eyes and bury us himself than give in to a threat. He might even be the first in line to take a plea deal or to get immunity to testify against us. Just out of spite. We need Haley. And the money."

Charlie met Seth's evil gaze. "Only one way I'll talk, if you're man enough for it."

No way she was going to make this easy for him. The fear was there, like a shadow in her soul, eclipsed now by the anger running through her like a cold iron bar. These might be the last minutes of her life. She wanted to spend them fighting.

"Cut her loose," Seth said, fury rife in his voice.

"Are you kidding?" Eklund asked. "You're going to fight her?"

"Why not?" Seth shrugged, slipping the switchblade in his pocket. "I've got no qualms about hitting a woman. Especially if means getting what we need. I'm happy to beat the answers out of her."

"This is beyond sadistic," Alcock said.

"Shut up." Seth stepped toward him. "Ortega is on the way here. We need to be the ones getting the answers. The ones showing that we're still in control. Not him."

"The cartel's rep is coming? I'm out of here." Alcock took off down the path toward his vehicle.

"Do you want me to go after him?" Colvin asked.

Seth shook his head. "Let the bottom-feeder go. He won't talk. Too much to lose. His license to practice law. His reputation. His picture-perfect family. All those luxuries he enjoys."

Eklund drew a bowie knife from a holster on his hip, sliced the zip tie around her wrists and shoved her forward.

The ground was cold and damp beneath her bare feet. The feel of the mud and grass grounded her. To get the circulation going, she shook out her arms, and then hopped up and down to warm up. Sparring with Rocco kept her nimble, her reflexes sharp.

Getting out of this alive wasn't her aim since the odds were slim. All she wanted was to give Seth hope. Hope that she'd cave under the pressure of violence. But she knew the truth. Nothing he did would work.

You couldn't break what was already broken. Her father had done the job a long time ago.

Her one goal was to use every punch and kick she threw to crush Seth's hope. And her only regret was that she hadn't told Brian that she loved him. She did. She'd thought it rash to say it. That it was too soon. She'd also been scared.

But now her greatest fear was that he'd never know how deeply she felt for him.

The car engine fired up. Tires sped down the road as Alcock fled from the farm.

"Did Haley ever tell you that I like it when my women fight back?" Seth asked. "Makes it more enjoyable. And my wife brought me a lot of pleasure. She was a scrapper, too."

Steeling herself, Charlie lifted her fists as she and Seth circled each other in the space between the barn and firepit. Eklund and Colvin drew their firearms but kept them low at their sides. Even if she won, they were going to make sure she didn't leave this farm alive.

With a feral smile, Seth lunged.

She deflected his fist and whipped her forearm upward as though she was smoothing back her hair. The tip of her bent elbow hit his chin, splitting the flesh to the bone.

Seth's head lashed back, blood ribboning from the wound, as he sucked in a breath.

Yes.

She needed this bastard to feel pain now. Not tomorrow.

Seth jabbed with one hand and swung a right hook.

Charlie feinted left, then threw a thunderclap to his ear with the heel of her palm. His eyes rolled into the back of his head, but he recovered quickly. She waited for him to retaliate defensively. When the blow came, she sidestepped.

But her attacker swung again and again. Each time he missed. Barely.

Once there was a break in Seth's momentum for her to capitalize on, she seized it. She threw a kick to his knee with her heel. He dropped to the ground with a grunt. Then she launched a punch, making contact with his eustachian tube at the hinge of his jaw, her knuckles sinking into the soft skin at the delicate spot. But she'd slipped too far inside Seth's reach.

Instantly, she realized the mistake would cost her dearly.

He caught her wrist. A switchblade flashed open, slashed up her arm, then down across her midsection. The fiery sting drew a ragged gasp from between her teeth.

"Never said it would be a fair fight, bitch."

Chapter Fifteen

A car raced down the road, leaving the ranch like a bat out of hell.

Brian and Kent ducked behind a stand of trees, ensuring they weren't spotted. Once the car tore out on the main road, another one approached the farm. A black SUV. Chevy. Moderate pace like the driver had all the time in the world.

His gut tightened. Brian double-checked the GPS app.

The blinking red dot was up ahead and not in the vehicle that had just left. "She's still here."

Kent gave him a thumbs-up.

"Come on," Brian said. They needed to hurry.

He and Kent pressed forward.

As they passed a black van, three pickups and the now parked SUV, a foul odor in the air grew stronger. Brian signaled Kent to go through the back door of the barn. If it was locked, then he'd have to ease around the left side. Either way, it'd not only give them two angles of coverage, but it would maximize the element of surprise.

Kent nodded and moved into position as silently as he could. Brian watched him tug at the back door to the barn.

In a back-and-forth slashing motion, Kent waved across his neck. *Locked.* He gestured to the left of the barn. Then keeping low and moving fast, he crept into the darkness, disappearing around a tree.

Going around the right side, Brian took stealthy, measured steps.

Seth was a seasoned police officer, which made him even more dangerous. If he or the other dirty cops with him heard or spotted Brian and Kent coming, there was nothing stopping them from killing Charlie.

The timing had to be just right. He hoped and prayed that nothing went wrong. The need to have Charlie safe and back in his arms was overwhelming.

His heart thundered so hard the frantic beats filled his ears until other sounds rose in the air.

Squeals. Grunts. The slap of flesh against flesh.

Pressure gathered in Brian's chest as a rush of adrenaline flooded his veins. With his back to the wall, he eased up to the corner of the barn, Glock drawn. He peered around the side, every muscle, every cell in his body coiled tight and ready.

Charlie.

She was alive. Standing in her underwear, blood streaked across her abdomen, her arm, she was in a defensive position, fists up. Horror screamed through him.

Seth was holding something that gleamed in the

firelight. A knife. Brian ached to blow a hole through him, but Charlie was in the way.

Colvin and Eklund both had guns drawn.

Brian wanted to leap into action that very second, but he needed to give Kent a chance to get into position on the other side of the barn. Otherwise, one of them might shoot her.

"If you don't get her to talk, I will," said the man with the ugly scar. "I'm rather good at it. Taking fingers. Toes. I guarantee once she smells her own flesh burning, she'll tell me all her secrets."

Tension knotted in Brian's chest, his heart throbbing like an open wound. He had to prevent that man from ever touching her and get her out of there.

Charlie threw a punch, her fist hitting Seth's jaw.

The big guy staggered back. "You're going to talk, so help me, even if I have to break every bone in your body." He kicked her in the gut, slamming her backward down onto the ground.

Waiting any longer wasn't an option. Brian took aim on the guy with the scar. He was the closest armed man to him and the scariest. His police training had taught him to go for center mass. But Special Forces had taught him sometimes you only had one shot to eliminate a threat. On an exhale, he squeezed the trigger.

A shot to the head. The man dropped.

But everyone else spun around, now on alert.

Quickly, he shot at Colvin, who was moving. Two bullets hit him. One in the arm. The other in the shoulder.

As Colvin aimed to return fire, Brian caught a glimpse of Charlie. She rammed the heel of her foot into Seth's groin and kicked the knife from his hand right before Brian took cover.

Bullets bit into the barn not far from his head.

On the other side of the building, gunfire erupted. *Kent.*

Ducking low, Brian darted out. Locked Colvin in his sights. Fired. The detective took one to the chest, lurched back and fell to the ground.

Seth pulled a gun and snatched Charlie by her hair, yanking her up in front of him. He hauled her back to the barn door. Flung it open. Dragged her inside at gunpoint.

Busy firing at Kent, Eklund hunkered down behind the stone firepit. He was too big to fully conceal himself, but a tree blocked Brian's line of sight for a clear shot.

Kent maneuvered off to the side behind a tractor.

"Cover me!" Brian called out, grateful for the extra ammo he'd given to him.

His partner squeezed off rounds, keeping Eklund pinned down and unable to shoot back.

Taking the small opening, Brian ran to the barn door and slipped inside. He stopped cold.

Seth had an arm curled around Charlie's throat, his gun pressed to back of her skull, her body shielding his. "Drop it. Or she's dead."

"Don't do it," Charlie said.

"I've had enough of you!" Seth growled, tightening his hold until she gasped.

Outside more gunfire was exchanged. Brian hoped that Kent could wear down Eklund, getting him to run out of ammo and then neutralize him.

Seth shifted the muzzle of his gun from the back of Charlie's head, jamming it against her temple. "Unless you want to see her brains splattered across the wall, you'll drop it."

Fury like Brian had never experienced surged inside him. Instead of suppressing it, he let it fill him, fuel him. If there was going to be a hostage, it would be him. He'd trade places with Charlie. His life for hers. He was willing to make any sacrifice. But first he made a solemn vow. "Hurt her again, and I will kill you."

"No, you won't," Seth said. "Not while I have her."

The gunfire outside stopped. Either Eklund or Kent was dead.

If it was the former, Kent would reposition around to the back of the barn, cutting off any escape for Seth. But if it was the latter, and his partner, his friend, was dead, Eklund would put a gun to the back of Brian's head, and this would be over.

He didn't glance over his shoulder. Instead, he focused on Charlie. Her face was bruised. She was covered in mud. Blood ran down her bare arm and stomach where she'd been cut. But there was something so hard and cold in her expression that it was startling.

"Me for her." Brian raised his hands. His finger off the trigger, but his grip still on the gun. "Let her go and take me instead."

"Brian." The intensity of Charlie's stare burned through him. Those green eyes were laser sharp. "Aim and pull the trigger." She tried to nod, but Seth's grip was too tight around her neck.

"Don't test me," Seth warned. "I will put a bullet in her."

The urge to beat this guy to a bloody pulp flared hot through Brian, but he stayed put. For Charlie's sake.

She clutched the arm at her throat, struggling to push it down. "I should've said this sooner. I love you." Her whispered admission cut through the barn, gutting him. "It's okay."

She was making the tough call, giving him permission to take the shot. To do his job.

But how could she think that he would risk her life? "No, Charlie. I can't." Not now. Not ever.

"You have to do it," she said, her voice like steel.

"Here's what's going to happen," Seth said. "I'm going to walk out of here with her. And you're not going to follow me.

"If he takes me," Charlie said, "I die anyway."

The ways this could play out right along with the odds had already gone through his head. Seth wasn't taking her anywhere. But he needed Charlie to trust that he had a plan.

"Toss your weapon!" Seth ordered.

Brian dropped it. His Glock landed on the barn floor with a thud.

"Kick it away!" Seth scurried toward the back of the barn with Charlie in tow. "Right now."

Brian swept the gun aside with his foot, sending it skidding into a dark corner.

Seth reached the back door and shoved on it, realizing it was locked. Moving the gun away from Charlie's temple, he popped the padlock with two bullets.

The door swung open. Kent, DCI Logan Powell, Chief Deputy Holden Powell and another deputy appeared on the other side.

Charlie thrusted backward, forcefully, giving Seth a sharp headbutt.

The violent blow over her skull to his face stunned him.

Brian bent down. Snatched the Beretta from his ankle holster.

Seth scurried backward into a corner, into the protection of two walls with Charlie as his shield. Before he could reposition the gun to her head, she sank her teeth into the arm around her throat. Seth howled in pain and slammed the butt of the gun down against her head.

Brian's stomach went into freefall as she went limp like a rag doll. Her deadweight tugged on him, forcing him to let her go. As she hit the ground, Seth turned the gun on her.

But Brian aimed and fired. He shot him twice in the throat, putting an end to him.

He hurried to Charlie, hauling her into his lap, cradling her head. "Open your eyes, honey."

She didn't move. Her skin cold and clammy, her face pale.

The other men charged inside. One checked Seth for a pulse.

Kent dropped to a knee beside him. "Is she—"

"No," Brian said. "But we need an ambulance."

But then her eyes fluttered open.

His heart squeezed with relief, and it was like he could breathe again.

Three days later

CHARLIE SAT ON Brian's lap in the living room, scrolling through the news article he'd wanted her to read.

She skimmed through the story.

According to the *Laramie Gazette*, Chief of Police Willa Nelson had finally issued a statement. A task force operating out of the DCI's office had been formed six months ago to look into the alleged ties between the Rios drug cartel, out of Mexico, and several police officers in key positions throughout the Laramie PD, as high ranking as Lieutenant Malcolm Jameson. The probe had started with a few narcotics detectives but had been expanded to include a huge array of civilians working in the organization. Real estate attorney Timothy Alcock had played a key role in using his legal expertise to help the cartel and officers create shell companies to hide behind in purchasing foreclosed homes to use as meth labs, and sites of storage and distribution. Charges included trafficking and selling drugs, prostitution, money laundering and racketeering. Based on DNA recovered from Olsen Ranch A, Detective Seth Olsen was also found to be responsible for several murders, including those of Theodore Williams and Jane Aubrey Dunn. The owner of the ranch, Abel Olsen, was not found to be complicit. An unidentified informant was key to breaking the case and turned over half a million dollars in cartel money. Chief Nelson has pledged to clean up the LPD.

"Wow," she said in a whisper. The informant was clearly Haley, who was still in an unidentified location. "I had no idea it was so big and deep. Are you all right?"

"Yeah."

But Brian was an idealist. He couldn't possibly be fine. "You can tell me."

He shook his head. "Those cops abused people and their positions. They violated the public trust in every way that counts. They've put a stain on the department that won't go away anytime soon."

Such a good man.

She kissed his head, pressed her palm to his cheek and ran her thumb over the evening stubble on his face. "Justice will be served. Take comfort in that. I'm just glad this nightmare is over."

"Me, too. But Chief Nelson still has a lot of work to do with the LPD."

She slid her fingers through his hair. "You know, I'm still surprised that you called Orson for help."

A smile pulled at his gorgeous mouth. "I'd do anything for you."

She believed him and was grateful to have Brian in her corner.

"I need you to do a favor for me tomorrow," he said.

"Anything. What is it?"

"Help me pick out a kitten. For Kent. I promised to buy him a cat."

Smiling, she kissed him again. This time on the lips. "It would be my pleasure."

Putting her down on her feet, he stood. "Go shower and meet me outside. I've got a surprise for you."

"What is it?"

He gently bopped her nose with the tip of his finger. "If I told you, then it wouldn't be a surprise."

"I thought we were having dinner."

"Food is a part of it."

"How long do I have?" she asked.

"As long as you need."

She frowned.

"Can you meet me out back in ten?"

"Sure," she said, but she'd do it in five.

She hurried through a shower, gritting her teeth every time the warm spray of water hit a scrape or bruise, and there were many. Exfoliating and shaving were musts since she was with Brian every night.

In a relationship.

The words still sounded weird in her head. Even weirder rolling off her tongue.

Wait until she told Rocco. He was going to lose his mind. In a good way.

She threw on Brian's T-shirt and padded down the hall.

The back door was open. The light on the porch was off. But a trail of candles lit a path.

Nerves fluttered in her stomach.

Smiling, she followed the candlelight out onto the lawn. Wearing his cowboy hat, Brian sat on a blanket that was surrounded by dozens of blazing candles. There was picnic basket, champagne flutes and bubbly.

She stepped on the blanket and sauntered over to him. "What are we celebrating?"

"Besides, being alive and being in love?"

She gave a little nod, her smile spreading wider.

Brian rose to his feet, then got down on one knee. "A proposal."

Her heart started pounding so loudly she could hear it.

He reached into his back pocket and pulled something out. But it wasn't a ring box. It was an envelope. "Open it."

She peeled back the flap that was sealed and took out two tickets. For the upcoming charity gala to support the women's shelter in Cheyenne. The same one they had gone to and found magic in each other. "I didn't realize this was in less than a week."

"Good thing I did. Charlie Sharp, will you be my date?"

She wanted to be his everything.

Funny how coming inches away from death, especially twice in one day, made her clearly see all the things lacking in her life.

Emotion ballooned inside her, but she refused to cry, even if they were tears of joy.

"Of course, I will."

He stood, put his hat on her head and wrapped

his arms around her, tugging her flush against him. "I love you."

Every time he said those three little words, her heart rolled over slow and dreamy in her chest.

She'd already shown Brian her soft underbelly more times than she liked, and quite honestly nothing in her life had ever felt as good as having that level of trust. So, she gave herself permission to say it and revel in how deeply she meant the words, without having a gun to her head. "I love you, too."

* * * * *

#2151 TARGETED IN SILVER CREEK
Silver Creek Lawmen: Second Generation • by Delores Fossen
A horrific shooting left pregnant artist Hanna Kendrick with no memory of
Deputy Jesse Ryland...nor the night their newborn son was conceived. But
when the gunman escapes prison and places Hannah back in his crosshairs,
only Jesse can keep his child and the woman he loves safe.

#2152 DISAPPEARANCE IN DREAD HOLLOW
Lookout Mountain Mysteries • by Debra Webb
A crime spree has rocked Sheriff Tara Norwood's quiet town. Her only lead
is a missing couple's young son...and the teacher he trusts. Deke Shepherd
vows to aid his ex's investigation and protect the boy. But when life-threatening
danger and unresolved romance collide, will the stakes be too high?

#2153 CONARD COUNTY: CODE ADAM
Conard County: The Next Generation • by Rachel Lee
Big city detective Valerie Brighton will risk everything to locate her
kidnapped niece. Even partner with lawman Guy Redwing, despite
reservations about his small-town detective skills. But with bullets flying and
time running out, Guy proves he's the only man capable of saving a child's
life...and Valerie's jaded heart.

#2154 THE EVIDENCE NEXT DOOR
Kansas City Crime Lab • by Julie Miller
Wounded warrior Grayson Malone has become the KCPD's most brilliant
criminologist. When his neighbor Allie Tate is targeted by a stalker, he doesn't
hesitate to help. But soon the threats take a terrorizing, psychological toll.
And Grayson must provide answers *and* protection to keep her alive.

#2155 OZARKS WITNESS PROTECTION
Arkansas Special Agents • by Maggie Wells
Targeted by her husband's killer, pregnant widow and heiress Kayla Powers
needs a protection plan—pronto. But 24/7 bodyguard duty challenges
Special Agent Ryan Hastings's security skills...and professional boundaries.
Then Kayla volunteers herself as bait to bring the elusive assassin to justice...

#2156 HUNTING A HOMETOWN KILLER
Shield of Honor • by Shelly Bell
FBI Special Agent Rhys Keller has tracked a serial killer to his small
mountain hometown—and Julia Harcourt's front door. Safeguarding his
world-renowned ex in close quarters resurrects long buried emotions. But
will their unexpected reunion end in the murderer's demise...or theirs?

HICNM0523

HARLEQUIN
PLUS

Try the best multimedia subscription service for romance readers like you!

Read, Watch and Play.

Experience the easiest way to get the romance content you crave.

Start your **FREE TRIAL** at
www.harlequinplus.com/freetrial.